A Leap

By the Author

The Fire was Here

The Ice Carriers

The Injury

The Masterpiece

The Secret

Anna Enquist

a Leap

TRANSLATED BY

Jeannette K. Ringold

The Toby Press

A Leap: Six Monologues

First English Edition 2009

The Toby Press LLC
POB 8531, New Milford, CT 06676–8531, USA
& POB 2455, London W1A 5WY, England

www.tobypress.com

First published in Dutch as *De Sprong* by De Arbeiderspers

ISBN 978 1 59264 258 8, *paperback original*

A CIP catalogue record for this title is available from the British Library

Typeset in Garamond by Koren Publishing Services

Printed and bound in the United States

Contents

I. Alma, *1*

II. Mendel Bronstein, *27*

III. and IV. Cato and Leendert, *37*

V. The Doctor, *51*

VI. ...And I am Sara, *61*

1. Alma

PLACE: *private residence at Auenburgergasse 2, Vienna*
TIME: *end of May 1906, early evening*
SCENE: *a sofa, a rather large table with an ashtray or a dish and a stack of mail on it, against the wall an open cabinet with wine bottles and glasses and stacks of music, a closed closet with coats, dresses, shoes, a drawer with letters, a suitcase*
SOUND: *while the audience is entering, the Nocturne in D flat, opus 27, no. 2 by Chopin is heard.*

The curtain opens during the last measures.

* * *

Alma enters (well after the final chord), reading music. "CHOPIN" is clearly visible on the cover (an old Peters edition?).

This was me. Chopin wrote this piece for me. If someone asked me: who are you? I'd run to the grand piano and play the *Nocturne in D flat*. That was me. Nothing to add.

And now?

Alma

I mustn't play too loud, that will wake up the girls. I have to restrain myself in the *fortissimo*, otherwise I'll have to start over again with lullabies and bedtime rituals. Who am I now? A mother.

Pulls a letter from her pocket.

I play that nocturne. I feel nothing. Chopin must tell me who I am. He is silent.

Sinks down on the sofa.

I had looked forward to it so much. Two weeks without him. Two weeks to study, to pull out my scores with impunity, to surround myself with my own music. When I find my own sound again I will have found myself.

Two letters per day. From Essen: "Rehearsed for five hours. Corrected parts for seven hours. My eyes hurt. Send me the notes for the scherzo. Third drawer on the left from the bottom. You have the key. Ate four slices of bread. Also send me the first version of the andante. I want to have the whole history of the sixth around me. Send everything by registered mail."

I am a wife now. One of those who knows exactly where her husband has left his glasses.

The way that nocturne ends—whispering, fading—while all the spent passion can be heard in it. Is that me? Certainly not, it isn't finished yet; I would still be right in the middle. I had reached the *con forza* of the transition phrase in my life. Right before the recapitulation of the theme. So much had still to come.

If only I could feel it.

Reads aloud.

"The percussion section is a disaster. You know that it can't be loud enough for me. Do have the special giant drum shipped; I'll try it one more time. Have it packed in wood shavings!! And quickly! Just imagine how impatiently I'm waiting for it!"

Do this. Send that. Write them. Visit her. I'm an agency, an office, a secretarial service.

Goes to the table where a copy of the Sixth Symphony is stacked. Leafs wildly through the score, almost pulls out the pages.

I do it lovingly. It is a privilege to serve a great artist like Mahler. To sacrifice everything for his art. Efface myself, become one with him, listen with his ears, think with his brain. That is my task. That's me.

I urge everyone in the house to be quiet. I put felt slippers on the children's noisy little feet. If it were possible, I'd stuff a wad of flannel in their mouths. In the kitchen they muffle the clanging of pans with dishtowels. Even when he is working in the garden cottage. I raise my finger as soon as someone shouts or screams. He likes to have the windows wide open. The idea of sound is almost more disturbing than the sound itself. I know how that is. I provide the beneficent silence from which his marvelous music is created.

Turns away from the table, sits down on the sofa.

I didn't care for it, in the beginning. His songs! Affected. Artificial. He overloaded me with scores. At any moment the bell would ring, and another messenger would be standing there with a package under his arm. I went through everything on the piano. It meant nothing to me.

When we were in a room together with other people, an electric field would be created between us. It seemed to crackle and burn! Positive and negative poles. Well, I don't really understand electricity. He stank. He repelled me. He attracted me in a way that no one yet had. I had to get away. And then I thought of him all night long. Aflame.

I ridiculed his music. Miserable melody, artificial simplicity, a contrived old-fashioned effect. Of course I didn't say it to him. But to others. So many men to choose from: heroes, gods, artists! They swarmed admiringly around me. And I worked. My piano sonata, my suite, my dear songs. When I was finished, I'd put on my coat with the fur collar and go out. Then I'd let myself be adored. I enjoyed the opera; I loved to be admired.

Mahler doesn't know how to dress. He gesticulates excessively and keeps pushing his glasses back on his nose. He can't pronounce the letter "r." Inside he is an old man. The fact that he's old in years makes no difference to me. So was Klimt, and yet I loved him immensely. He painted me while I played for him. Through my music I drew him to me, just as he drew me to him with his paintings. It can happen like that! Except that it couldn't—I was too young; he had one woman after the other; my family wouldn't put up with it.

Gustav couldn't touch me with his art as directly as Klimt did. Something was amiss; I didn't know where he started from. And I hate what he loves. Mountain scenery. Country air. Nature.

When I first looked at the score of his *First Symphony*, I didn't understand it at all. An undulating sea of chords with here and there an oboe or horn screaming above it like the screech of a bird. And then the much too cheerful theme of the first part. A fresh spring morning in the meadows, tralala, yo-ho, into the woods!

Sings the theme.

I hate being outdoors. There are no boundaries; everything runs together; it doesn't stop. I'm much more at ease between four walls. Moreover, the heater can be on. I want nothing to do with a starry sky above me. I prefer the piano lamp. A music room with heavy carpets and velvet curtains. The only light falls on my own hands. If need be, the stairs of the Opera House with its chandeliers and gilded balustrades. As long as there is a roof and I can feel enclosed and held. I like it when air is limited, when everyone breathes the same oxygen, when the smells don't disperse.

When I'm tired, I close the windows and lie down on the sofa with my nose in the pillows. Gustav goes outside. To walk, he says. He means to run, to clamber, to climb. For days on end. He has a filthy, sweaty bag on his shoulders and eats bread with apples. He spends nights in small primitive inns and sends me overly enthusiastic letters: how refreshing, how restful, how grand.

And that he misses me.

Without me he gets nothing done. From the first moment he knew that I was the one he was lacking. Why? In his eyes I was a silly goose. He barely heard me play. That doesn't interest him at all. He has never seen a note of my music. Not interested. I loved to chat, to drink, to dance. He detests that. Yet he knew that he had to have me. And he was right!

I was in love with Zemlinsky. My Alex. He valued my compositions and pored over them more than anyone else did. He became fired with enthusiasm when I played for him. Where is he, by the way? He knows that I'm alone here. Why doesn't he visit me? I treated him heartlessly. I wounded him deeply. So strange, I loved him dearly. As soon as Gustav appeared on the stage, I dropped Alex. Who is the greater artist—that's what it's about. Subconsciously I must have realized that Mahler was the master. He called me. I came. It was as simple as that.

At first I didn't realize it. I continued to write my song cycle diligently and practiced my counterpoint exercises. It isn't easy to put aside a life's calling. I was my music. I saw myself in the future as a pianist, as a composer, as a conductor! My thoughts have always been melodies, and I experience everything I do in a rhythmic cadence. I *am* music—*my* music. And then a man comes into my life who has the nerve to ask me to give all that up. Asks? No, demands!

Actually, nothing has ever shocked and confused me as did Gustav's letter of conditions. Twenty incredible pages. I couldn't believe what I was reading.

Recites radiant, happy. This whole passage in a moving, joyful tone.

"I don't want to talk about your music. Do you think that you're renouncing something indispensable if you give it up to be mine?

What kind of 'work' are you talking about? Composing, perhaps? The role of composer is *mine. I*'m the one who works, let there not be any misunderstanding about that. Your role is to give up all superficial pastimes—like your so-called work—to make yourself completely and unconditionally subordinate to my needs. You should not desire anything else except my love."

That night I read his letter at least twenty times. I paced up and down my room, moaning, at my wit's end. Giving up my music seemed inconceivable, and Gustav's demand seemed to imply an outrageous intimacy, as if he were proposing that I have my breasts amputated. At the same time it was also intoxicating, seductive, inexplicably flattering. He loved me so much that he wanted to maim, destroy, kill me. More is not possible.

Mama came upstairs. She had become worried because of my stomping and running about. I let her read the letter and remained standing in front of her with my hands folded until she was finished. "Tsk, tsk, tsk," she went, shaking her head from time to time. No, she doesn't get it, I thought. This love is beyond her.

She became furious. "Slavery," she said, "meddling, extreme egotism. You must give up this man, Alma. You have to break it off with someone who fails to appreciate you to such an extent. Break it off! Tomorrow!"

I saw the red spots on her neck flare up. With her knees pressed together, she sat on the edge of my bed and leafed with trembling fingers through the batch of writing paper. "You've made music all your life," she said, "how can you stop that? No person should ask that of another. How does he get it into his head, that Mahler? Is he that much better than anyone else?"

The longer Mama rattled on, the more clearly I felt a stillness descend in my body. I suddenly realized that I possessed a treasure that I could give him. I had never felt as powerful and noble. What was Mama actually talking about? What did she understand about passion, about sacrifices? I became perfectly calm. With slow, careful movements I took the letter from her lap, folded it, and put it in a drawer. That's where it still is. I thanked Mama for her advice and said that I was going to sleep. Resolute, serene. Saved.

Now I need a drink.

Takes a bottle from the cupboard, pours, drinks quickly.

I felt like a kind of saint. I brought a magnificent sacrifice to the altar of love, of art. Too bad that he had no idea of the nature of that sacrifice. But that made it perhaps even more impressive.

Before I went to bed, I wrote him a short letter. "I am completely yours. Outside of your needs and wants nothing is of any interest to me. My dearest wish is to devote myself completely to you and your music."

Then I went to sleep, deep and dreamless. Everything was good.

The next day I gathered my manuscripts and scores and put them in the morocco leather bag that Alex had given me. I even added the pieces of scrap paper with counterpoint exercises. For a moment I toyed with the idea of celebrating by burning everything in the big fireplace in the salon. Wouldn't Gustav be moved and surprised when I used my opera drafts as kindling, pushed my songs into the fire with the poker, threw my sonatina into the flames? A wave of proud warmth flowed through me when I thought of the amount of love that would have to become a counterweight to this.

I hid the bag in the back of a closet and showed Gustav my empty desk when he came. He was elated. News of the engagement leaked out, and congratulations telegrams and bouquets were delivered. Mama walked around with pursed lips and a frown on her low forehead. Gustav and I wrestled through a four-handed version of his *Fourth Symphony*. He gave me the score as his engagement present. Solemnly I placed the stack of huge sheets on my table, on the spot where until then my own work had lain. "I prefer Haydn," I said. He laughed.

I think that he was happy those first weeks after my sacrifice. In the evenings I accompanied him to the Opera and watched closely how he conducted. Before starting, he looked for my face in the loge. He is very near-sighted.

I remember receptions, soirees, banquets. Despite her objections to our engagement, Mama had two gorgeous dresses sewn for me. I had ordered a new corset and had bought lily-white satin underwear. I wanted to be pure and noble.

Thank God, to everyone's surprise, Justi, his stern sister, had acquired a lover, so she lacked the energy to play chaperone when I'd visit Gustav. I simply walked to his work room and could spend hours there undisturbed while she walked through the park with her boyfriend. Usually Gustav would start by showing me scores. That was the most intimate thing he could show me. I didn't care for it at all. Music from before my time. I stood outside his world of sound, and that bothered me. I wanted to get in.

Soon we'd be sitting on the edge of his couch with a wobbly stack of music in our laps. My shoulder rested against his: I didn't draw back but increased the pressure almost unnoticeably. The heat that emanated from that man. I registered everything. The throat clearing. The steamed-up glasses. The slips of the tongue. The trembling fingers. *My* work.

Why didn't I get excited? My intellect is too strong. I kept watching and observing. Exasperating. When he talked fast, I saw white spittle in the corners of his mouth. With a flourish I swept the music sheets to the floor. To business!

Then I could lose myself; I wanted to be totally absorbed in him. Or rather he in me…

Oh well. All those details. Much ado about nothing—let me leave it at that. He couldn't manage and lay crying from shame and humiliation. I heard Justi's key in the front door. Take it or leave it, I thought. I was a noble, sacrificing woman who didn't hold anything against her lover. Alex's wild lover, out for her own pleasure, had disappeared; I no longer knew myself.

The next few days Gustav had an unbearable migraine. Justi

walked back and forth with ice bags and painkillers. The doctor was called. I visited Gustav for a short time and placed a cool hand on his mighty forehead. It was rather cool outside, and I had forgotten my gloves. "Oh Almschi, Almschili, I'm so sorry," he moaned.

Justi let me out and told me in a whisper that the doctor had prescribed ice cold sitz baths because of an unhealthy blockage in the lower abdomen.

That's what you get.

I persisted, and when we got married I was pregnant. God knows how I managed to do that, but it worked. My body protested, for I was sick every morning and hung puking above the sink. My new corset no longer fit, but that didn't bother me. Something, someone was consuming me from inside. I no longer was myself. Gustav was proud. He beamed. He seemed to grow, and I shriveled up. After the vomiting sessions, when he ran off to the Opera for the morning rehearsal, I sat down at the piano sighing and waited until I felt like playing a triad. I felt nothing. My hands were swollen and felt uncomfortable, strange. Then I lay down again until he called that he was coming to eat.

Those meals! Those stormy walks afterwards! He forced me to walk the whole Ring in a murderous tempo. It's a wonder that I didn't have a miscarriage. I swelled. I no longer talked to anyone. I had given up everything. I had become an incubator.

No one had prepared me for childbirth. Who should have done that anyway? I no longer spoke with Mama; she looked at me reproachfully when we saw each other and didn't ask me once how I felt. I didn't flinch. Justi had never been pregnant, and of course Gustav had no clue. The doctor, his hand already on the door handle, said only how wonderful childbirth was. A wonder, every time. "Don't worry, Madame, nature takes its course and we merely have to submit to it."

That should have made me suspicious. Nature. I don't know anything more cruel and more uncomfortable.

To endure pain is manageable; if I know how it comes about

and that it will pass I can manage it quite well. During my most painful periods I composed the most beautiful songs. Pain is a challenge. It opens the path to the inner world. Pain is a friend; you can defy it or you can surrender to it. This pain was different—it was impossible to cope with. Even worse was the powerlessness. How I was lying on that high bed, how they strapped me in chilly stirrups, how they tore the child out of me and carelessly destroyed everything that was in their way.

When it was finally over, a nurse held the swaddled, blue baby in front of my face and expected me to melt with happiness. I thought of the pedal action for the nocturne, how you can take that entire pianissimo passage with its beautiful grace notes practically on one pedal if you do it carefully. In the measure before *con anima* you have to change twice. My right ankle moved in the stirrup.

They washed me. Gustav came in. He cried and held the child close. His daughter. Her name had to be Maria, after his mother, even though he couldn't say the *r*.

He was changed by the birth of the child; he needed me less now that he was a father. He went whistling off to his work and the one or two times that I managed to drag my ailing body to the Opera, I saw him hanging around the soprano, chattering and cooing.

"Otherwise she can't sing," he said when I furiously reproached him for flirting. I turned away and thought of Alex, who understood me. Sometime, later, I would—I don't know what I thought.

I couldn't love the child. It was his. "Where is my Puti-Puti-Putschi?" he'd shout as soon as he came home. I had never been so lonely. I couldn't find the way back to my music; first someone had to love me. I had to have friends again. But Gustav couldn't stand that.

He became engrossed in a multiple birth. I heard new themes turn up in his whistling and humming. I got hold of myself. If I couldn't write anything myself, I would be the midwife for his compositions. I could lace my corset up again. I demanded company. Friends came again. Gustav caught me in an embrace with some fool or other. Reconciliation. Tears.

We spent the summer in Maiernigg. The house was surrounded by dark trees. When you'd go outside, there was nature. Gustav sat in his composing cottage in the woods and I waited in the gloomy room for his commands. When he had written enough, he'd run downstairs, strip out of his clothes, and shouting, plunge into the lake. Then I had to come and watch him swim. His shoes stood near the boathouse, his glasses in the right shoe. His wet hair was plastered flat against his head. He climbed onto the landing and lay naked in the sun. That was healthy, he said. He peered in my direction. Without glasses he sees nothing.

I sat on a rock, my knees pulled up. What had I become? Where was my life? He turned over. Pale buttocks in the sun. There is no way out.

He grabbed my foot and tried to loosen the buckle of my shoe. He showered my instep with kisses. My stockings became wet. Slowly I set my parasol down on the grass.

Then the deal was made.

The sun moved behind the trees and I looked at the small patches of light that danced on the water. At the horizon rose the stark silhouette of the Karawanken mountains. This landscape did not take the slightest notice of me. The water would continue to lap at the shore, the trees would continue to extend their branches, the mountain tops would soak up the sun every evening; whether I was there or not made no difference. I became afraid. Nature seemed to me like an audience that ignored me. I don't like that.

Meanwhile Gustav was talking to my calves. He is someone who tolerates nature, even loves it and needs it. "Get dressed," I wanted to say, "I don't want that wildness." But I remained silent. In the big house the baby had surely awakened from her afternoon nap. Oh well, that's what servants are for. My place was here, on the damp landing next to the naked artist.

A symphony, he said. About me, for me, thanks to me. He did not want to write another note that wasn't inspired by me. My music would come alive in his. He had noticed that it bothered me when he was working on ideas from before my time, themes from before.

That was over. He was going to devote himself to me just as I devoted my life to him. Because this magnificent coin had another side. He took my face between his cold hands and gave me a piercing look. Just as a symphony from me would come into being in him, so a child from him would start to grow in me. We would become pregnant with each other's seed, our ovaries would start to swell through an unparalleled artistic-biological cross-pollination, in time resulting in a sublime double accomplishment.

"Almschi," he said, "I already have the theme of the andante in my head. It occurred to me when I was lying in the water and looking at the mountains. It's about the noblest thing in you: your motherhood!"

That's how it happened. At the end of the summer he had written two parts of the symphony and I was pregnant. I really wanted to believe in our plan. Gustav sat in his composing cottage and I stood behind the window. The whole house smelled of applesauce; in the kitchen they were canning and preserving. I waited. When I saw him coming outside, I sent Maria to him. Father and daughter ran toward each other, shouting, waving their arms. Gustav took a leap and lifted the child high above his head. She went limp; her fat little legs dangled in front of his face. Then he carried her in his arms and danced wildly through the high grass. Lifting his legs high, he sang and stamped in a strange rhythm. The child had bright-red cheeks from excitement. I watched.

That evening he handed me my shawl and took me to the cottage. There was dew on the grass. Arm in arm we walked into the darkness. He squeezed my hand.

On the table lay a mountain of music paper, handkerchiefs, open scores, a shriveled apple, a glove. Gustav sat down at the piano and started playing his scherzo for me. At each entry he called out the instruments at the top of his voice: "Horns! Here the oboe! Strings, more intensity!! Bass tuba!" He hammered out a series of low As on the rickety piano. The rhythm shifted, it seemed as if there were two first counts played again and again, and it made me think of the frenetic stomping dance on the grass. He had danced the scherzo with the child.

I lowered my head and looked intently at the music that lay on the table. A corner of the yellowish paper that he used to use stuck out of a stack. I pulled at it and read: *Kindertotenlieder.* There were corrections in between the previously written passages. On the next page I recognized Gustav's recent handwriting. I pulled at the stack while Gustav was pounding out his scherzo. He had composed two new lieder. Now. This summer. Without saying anything.

"I wanted to have it finished," he said softly. "Now it's done. From now on I'll write only for you."

I cloaked my anger in fear. "When your children are healthy you shouldn't write about their deaths," I said. "You'll call fate down on yourself." Did he know me so little that he believed these words? Maybe. I don't think that he understood why I was so intolerant of his writing about his daughter. Men's jealousy is different.

He certainly understood that I was displeased. "Do go and play again, Almschel. Maria sleeps; I work; you have plenty of time. Shall I have the piano tuner come?"

I shrugged my shoulders. What sense does it make to practice if I can't compose? If I can't speak about what I'm working on? If I'm not allowed to take lessons? If I'm not allowed to see Alex?

Gets up, pulls a suitcase from the closet.

I have to pack. Travel. Dress rehearsal. Opening performance. Take jewelry? The drafts! The score!

Places these items on the table.

Gustav will be a bundle of nerves. At the last moment he'll want to let an oboe play with the strings somewhere; he'll want to scrap or change an incredibly difficult passage that a trombonist has practiced for weeks; he'll hesitate about the position of the percussion section; he'll need me. The brown or the blue one?

Holds up two dresses; drops both of them into the suitcase.

Shoes.

Bends down to the bottom of the closet; straightens herself, holding a leather bag.

Open it, take the music out and place it on the table. My music. Do I dare? He's not here; the children are asleep; no one sees me.

Oh well, it's too late. Too many years have passed.

Places the bag on the table.

That second pregnancy was easier for me, but I didn't let on. I stuck out my belly and planted my hands on my back. "Shooting pains," I moaned, "headache, malaise." The sofa in the salon became my territory. Visitors had to sit in straight-backed chairs, and I stretched out my legs on pillows. Yes, visitors! Gustav was worried about me and consulted a physician. "She needs diversion," said the doctor, "to be part of the world. Take her to the theater, invite friends, bring life inside if she can't go out!"

Gustav's face clouded over. His idea of a healthy pregnancy was total isolation, relieved by running through the Belevedère Park. Now, on doctor's orders, he had to allow me in the warm salon to engage in conversation with men who had perhaps come for him but who were mainly interested in me. "It is difficult to develop in a melancholy mother," said the doctor. "Do think of the child!"

He agreed, and finally I saw my Alex again. He has no chin, he's an ugly frog, but I've never seen such sweet and passionate eyes. He came together with Schoenberg; Gustav sat with them impatiently, but he didn't walk out. I felt embarrassed about my shape and lay on the sofa with closed eyes. The low mutter of the men's voices was a blessing.

That winter Gustav traveled often. That's when I tried to play the piano, but I could no longer cross my arms in front of my belly. One afternoon I was sitting despairing at the keyboard when Alex was shown in. I hadn't heard the door bell at all. I had kicked off my shoes. Swollen feet. He saw my tears, came and stood behind me, and placed his hand on my neck.

That's how it began in the past. When he was my teacher. While I played I felt his body. First the presence, then the warmth, and finally the pressure. He folded his arms around my breasts. I stopped playing, fortunately at a point where I could easily modulate to the tonic by attaching a final chord to it, and leaned with my head against his chest. I let him have his way. He played me passionately. I reached a crescendo.

Rummages in the bag, pulls out a sheet of music.

After he left, I feverishly wrote a short song that said everything. Precisely as it was. A chromatic rising melody, first hesitant, but then more urgently to a climax. Then a sigh of fulfillment. It was on paper within fifteen minutes; I didn't need to change anything. Perfect. At the next lesson I played it.

Hums the beginning of the song.

He understood immediately what it was about. He blushed and kissed my hands.

Places bag and music on the table next to the Mahler scores.

I must stop those memories. It will never again be like before. Alex knows that I'm alone. Two weeks. He hasn't come. He hasn't written. I have to travel to Essen to hear the *Sixth Symphony. My* symphony. Written in exchange for a child.

She was born in June, after that desperate winter. It was glorious weather, the air was still, and the birds were singing. I let her go without any resistance. When the doctor came, she was already out, lively and independent. I lay in bed, exhausted; it had gone so quickly that I barely realized what had happened. I had Gustav called out of the morning rehearsal. He came into the room perspiring. "Mother, little mother," he whispered into my neck. Then he sang the theme of the andante, his ode to my motherhood. How annoyed I get by his manner of singing. Pedantic. Too emphatic.

Hums the beginning of part 3 in Gustav's manner.

The new baby lay on a pillow. Her name is Anna, I said. I hadn't thought about it, it just slipped out of my mouth. Putzi's name is Maria, after his mother. This new daughter is mine and is named after my mother.

The doctor wanted to have the curtains closed. I had to sleep. He had the child taken to another room and pushed Gustav out. I heard them move around in the hall. I was alone. Wide awake. Alert. Sleeping was out of the question. I heard Gustav and Maria talking to each other in the kitchen in high, clear, loud voices. From the distance a new sound could be heard: a reedy crying. Anna. I called for the nurse. Now they had to notify my mother. It was time for a reconciliation.

Mama had remained critical about my marriage. The birth of Maria had changed nothing. When she visited us, she looked past me. She was reserved to Gustav, although she did inquire about his work. She asked me once if I was sorry. If I missed my music. We were standing in the kitchen. She had brought jars of cherry jam, wrapped in old newspapers. She unwrapped the jars carefully and handed them to me.

Her question made me blush. I reached deep into the cupboard to put away a jar. The bare shelves echoed my voice. "No!" I shouted. "No, no, no."

Afterwards there was perfunctory contact for months. My

mother did not believe in my capacity to eat only lentils and apples, in my willingness to make sacrifices, in my motherhood.

I was nursing Anna when Mama came in. She remained standing at the door, wearing a coat and a ridiculous hat with feathers. To my surprise there were tears in her eyes. I placed my free hand around the baby's head—a small melon, a coconut.

"I named her after you," I said. Mama put away her hat and sat down with us. She seemed proud and pleased. I had passed the mother exam—I understood it! And she was right too. I could not love the first one. She had hurt me at her birth; she had not wanted to drink from my breast; at the first opportunity she had left me in the lurch in order to latch onto her father. This one was mine. I buttoned up my clothes and smiled. Mama smiled back.

We sent Gustav to Maiernigg. The sęason was finished and he was bursting with desire to continue working on his Sixth. I packed a large trunk for him: a summer suit, straw hat, walking shoes. The score he carried himself. Maria was inconsolable when he left. It's never soon enough to get used to your father's disappearance. Mine died when I was twelve years old. He left me behind with my selfish mother and her stupid friend. It hardened me. Scar tissue is stronger than vulnerable skin. Why doesn't the child get angry? Anger is infinitely more productive than sadness. She couldn't. I saw in her quiet little face that that she was stricken with loss; I thought of the wild dance of father and daughter on the grass and shrugged my shoulders.

After the birth of the oldest I had, to my horror, been unable to sit, to lift, or even to relieve myself. Every movement hurt, my body was run-down and worn. It is a curse to be a woman.

How different it was this time! I recovered miraculously fast and soon climbed up and down the stairs. Mama abandoned her household and moved in with us as soon as Gustav had left on the train. Carefree weeks.

The andante with the steady mother theme is in E-flat. No key is farther removed from A, the tonic of the other parts. He stuffs so much drama and despair into this symphony that he needs a classical framework to hold everything together. A major, A minor, open and brilliant, muffled and ominous. Keys that suit me. But E-flat? Can he sense that my motherhood is separate from me? Perhaps he has looked more closely at me than I think. Of course not, what nonsense. He raises the andante high above ordinary life by his choice of key. He is such an idealistic mother worshipper. He loves images of the Virgin Mary; he loves Maria.

He wrote me almost daily letters with lots of exclamation marks. "Tormented by a horrible headache!! So many themes in my head, but I don't manage to write them down! If only my Almschel were here, then I'd have peace! Make my existence complete, come quickly with our sweet daughters! I now know that I can't do without you!! Come!!!"

I miss him especially when he is present. When he sits across from me at the table and chews his whole wheat bread thirty times before swallowing—then I miss him.

I took my time. The children had colds, little Anna had a stuffy nose and couldn't nurse. I had a nasty cracked nipple and had to rest a lot. Mama took care of us and eventually decided to travel with us to Maiernigg. Four women for Gustav!

He looked pale, I thought. He had also lost weight. And dirty! His collar was greasy and his pants were covered with stains. We flung open our suitcases and released the smell of soap and talcum powder. Maria rushed outside to pick flowers. Mama disappeared into the kitchen, and it started to smell of roasted meat.

We were barely there one day when he started writing again. I cleared off the big table in the salon and started to copy out the scherzo. I did the orchestra parts as well, very carefully and intently. I enjoyed my own musical notation. So firm. So elegant.

One evening, as I was still copying out the second trumpet part, he came and stood behind me. "I want to let you hear something, Almschi. I've tried something—I'm really happy with it myself, but you have to say what you think of it." He pulled me up at my elbows. Mama was doing embroidery under the lamp and nodded at us. We left the house. I saw a light on in the composing cottage.

Gustav put his arm around me. We walked across the grass, finally in step with each other. I placed my arm across his thin back. He didn't rush me; he adjusted to my pace without complaining.

At the piano he seemed almost shy. He was working on the first part, he said as he looked at the keyboard. The second theme was about me. He had tried to capture my nature in a melody. My radiant zest for life, he said. My youth, my enthusiasm. Who I was. He played.

Sings the beginning of the Alma theme.

My melody would pervade the whole opening part of the symphony, push all other themes aside, and crop up everywhere. "Because you are my whole existence," he said. "I want to demonstrate that; I want to let it be heard. What do you think of it?" He got up and walked back and forth, wringing his hands. I was moved. A magnificent theme. It reached higher and higher; it plunged down and then flew up again with renewed force—higher, even higher! After the last passionate climax came the fall, a breakneck flight into the depths, to kettledrums and trombones. I was dazzled. I raised my head and kissed him. "Perfect," I said, "you captured me perfectly."

That night he slept with me and I no longer missed him.

I wanted to come to my senses while he was in Essen. Who am I if I am not his? I need the other like a mirror, otherwise I can't believe in myself. I played for Klimt: I composed for Alex. If Gustav portrays me in his theme, then I exist. I disappear if they don't desire me!

That summer he worked himself to death. The finale of his, of our, symphony expanded daily. A terrifying piece, somber, despairing. He suffocated every positive thought in furious percussion cannonades. I thought I heard the reflection of his cherished mountain walks in the cowbells and in the lively marching tempo, but he thought that was too limited. "I don't render events into music," he said. "The finale is about how it is. I can't explain it. Life. My life."

The music disturbed me. Before I knew it, the natural peace between us had disappeared. Every day I worked on the first part of the score, and each time I was struck by the resilience of my theme. Filled with admiration and love I copied out the parts for the violin, the oboe, and the bass tuba. I saw myself appear everywhere: in inversions, in *ritardando*, in fragments. I felt how I was part of Gustav's work. So I should be able to understand the finale. I did my best, but he made it difficult for me.

The turmoil of the finale seemed to get to me. I snapped at the children and started to be irritated at Mama again. I longed for Vienna. If only Gustav would go back to the Opera to conduct Beethoven; if only that miserable symphony were finished. In the autumn sun I would stroll through the city and would encounter old friends. I would no longer let myself be imprisoned; I would insist that I be allowed to receive whomever I wanted. Isn't it strange that Klimt, my first real love, is also called Gustav? Old love doesn't decay.

One morning Gustav came into the room unexpectedly. Cold air hung around him, and small drops stuck to his hair. "It is finished," he said. He embraced me. The children started to dance around us and to shout with joy, and Mama put away her embroidery. Completed. Done. Finished. He looked happy. I did my best to be happy too. The next day we started packing. Home!

A tragedy. We had barely arrived in Vienna when Mama managed to tell me that Klimt was getting married. Klimt! Marry! I remained calm but I seethed inside. He did it because he was pressed for money, I was sure of that. But it rankled. I can't stand being forgotten. I forced Gustav to go and eat out in the city with me at least once a week. Receptions, vernissages. He behaved disgustingly and made it abundantly clear that he was bored to tears. He killed every conversation with his overwhelming silence.

I started to receive again. He was angry and jealous, but I went ahead. Would I dare to invite Alex? Gustav liked him but couldn't stand the thought that he had been my lover. I wrote: "Gustav has completed his Sixth; come and see the new baby!"

And then both of my men were sitting next to each other at the grand piano. The piano excerpt lay on the music stand. I was standing behind the door. From the vehement touch of the marked eighths in the overture I could hear that Gustav must be sitting on the left and was playing the bass parts. That meant that Alex would soon introduce my theme! I trembled. How would it have been if I could have chosen Alex? Would I then have made an opera instead of two children? To live beside a man who loves not only me but also my work, what would that be like? Would I be able to compose if he encouraged and admired me? What would I create if there were no resistance?

Later that evening Schoenberg came by. Gustav and he had a vehement discussion in the salon, bent over the score. Alex sat down next to me without saying anything. The silence was more revealing and more dangerous than a public embrace. Alex seemed to sense that. "I've now heard what your husband has been doing," he said, "but what has come from your hands? Where is your music?" I blinked in order to control my tears.

Finally they left and rummaged in the hall with their coats and their briefcases. Alex grabbed my hand. "One word, Alma, one word, and I'll come and get you." Before I realized what he had so passionately whispered in my ear, the door had fallen shut.

Gustav didn't notice my confusion at all during the weeks that followed; that's how involved he was in what was happening with his symphony. Through Schoenberg's and Zemlinsky's enthusiasm he had become so convinced of the worth of his work that he very consciously played two publishers off against each other and received an enormous sum for the symphony. I was able to make up the deficits in our household funds and have a dress made. I sang lullabies to the children, did my copying in a disciplined manner, and created the menu every day. Meanwhile I fantasized about a future with Alex. My heart raced double time. I no longer slept.

The orchestra offered Gustav a play-through of the whole symphony. Eighty musicians were going to devour and spit out my theme. Gustav was thrilled. He was going to meet with the percussion section; he ordered a series of cowbells and had a drumhead stretched over an enormous crate. The big drum wasn't loud enough for him. When the monster came from the workshop, we went to the hall to witness the wonder. The first kettledrummer waved two enormous clubs through the air and let them come down with force on his marvelous creation. A dull thud without any resonance. I burst out laughing. Raging, Gustav stormed onto the stage and snatched the clubs from the kettledrummer's hands. He took a swing. *Bam, bam.* Then they pulled out the big drum again.

After the reading rehearsal Gustav started correcting again. He made so many changes that I had to start writing a clean version. I almost burned up the whole symphony. By accident. The oil lamp fell over and caused a flame that spread extremely fast over the sofa and the carpet. For a moment I stood riveted, as if the fire proclaimed my freedom. Then I started to scream and to throw blankets on the flames. The children were asleep in the adjoining room.

I have to go to Essen. Everything has to be in order.

Picks up the Mahler scores and places them in the suitcase, sits down again, takes a sip.

What am I actually doing? Do I want to do what I'm doing? I think I'm not doing what I want to. My will is concealed behind my actions. Or not?

Takes a stack of unopened mail from the table and starts tearing open envelopes.

Bills. That will come later.

Throws the letters back on the table. Keeps two and opens one of them.

No, Oh no. My dear Alex!

Reads aloud.

"Alma, you've been alone for a considerable time. I have not come by. You have composed and reflected, I hope. I have as well. My admiration for your husband and his work is immense. My love for you is even greater. There are now two possibilities. One: Pack a suitcase with some travel clothes and your work and come to me. We'll leave this very evening and will not return. The other: We each go our own way. I will never bother you again, and you will burn this letter. Tonight I will know which you have chosen. Your Alex."

Starts unpacking the suitcase very slowly. Then places the bag with her own compositions inside the suitcase and adds the Chopin nocturnes.

Where to? A villa in Venice, a small palace in Prague? Work! And in the evening tell each other what we've created. Play for him. Know that he is curious about my new song. Sit at the piano all day long without fear. Be admired for what I do, for what I write. I thought his last ballet was poor. He needs a muse. What am I saying? I love him! And he loves me! Has for years! He knows my talent better than anyone and will do everything to let it flower.

What if nothing comes and I'm not productive?

Oh, nonsense. That can't be.

I've been caged for so long that I'll penetrate all corners of the world once I'm released. My life starts now. I feel it. A decision.

Sinks down again, drinks, finds the second letter on the couch, reads aloud.

"Come on time, Almschel, I want you to be at the dress rehearsal. The hotel is fabulous; we're getting a suite. There is a very talented Russian pianist here, Gabrilovitch; he'd love to meet you. I'm considering placing the andante before the scherzo. What do you think? Come! Come quickly!!"

Gets up, unpacks the suitcase again. Mahler's music into it, hers out. Holds a match to Alex's letter, which she burns in the ashtray. Goes to the door with big steps and swinging her suitcase while singing the theme.

11. Mendel Bronstein

Rotterdam, the psychiatric hospital Maasoord, 1912

For forty years I lived in a spruce forest. It encircled the village; its darkness pressed against the windows; with nasty needles it pricked into my skin when I walked into the house round the back.

I was a tailor; with pins and darning needles I pierced through cloth and leather; I joined what was loose; I created what farmers' wives or neighbors thought up.

Water played no role, the widest stream could be bridged with a tree trunk. I had never seen an ocean, not even in my dreams.

I did what had to be done. I carried out my trade; I visited the small *shul*; I associated with my co-religionists and was polite to the others. And there was Helga. I had sewn her first small winter coat, of black wool—her blonde, copper curls against it! Later she came to work for me. For years she made my breakfast and swept my floors. It wasn't until she wanted to leave that I started to think about distance, vastness, spaciousness in the world.

There were more and more people who left. Often there was

no synagogue service because too few men came. There is no more work, they said. Harassment, name-calling, vandalism, prohibitions. I still had enough customers. And I had Helga.

They left with their chests and suitcases, their bundles and babies. A new century, a new land. I stayed.

Until Helga stood in front of me in her gray-green apron. I was making buttonholes in a man's coat. She could no longer stay and work for me; her father didn't like it, she said.

If I showered her with wages, if I married her, I wanted to ask. She looked at her shoes; I saw the top of her copper-blonde head. She left.

A film of dust spread over the floor, over the bales of wool and velvet, on the windowsills. It was difficult to think about eating, and I noticed that my clothes hung around my body. I hadn't gone to *shul* for a long time. I worked day and night, although no one bought my pants and coats anymore.

A man came to tell us about America. I went to listen; I hadn't left the house for days. Did I hope to see Helga? Did I really think about emigration? With her? I don't know anymore. I stood in the back of the small dark hall and listened as if it were an order. The next morning I sold everything that was in my workshop. For my money the American man gave me a boat ticket and a trip to the harbor of Rotterdam. Harbor, I thought, water, sea.

I left without seeing Helga. I admit that I waited a whole evening for her, hidden under a spruce. I saw the lights in her house go out one by one.

From my inventory I took with me only my best scissors and my case with needles. My informant had told me that there was plenty of work for competent tailors in America. I wore fairly new boots and had sewn the rest of my modest capital in the lining of my coat. Warm and rustling. Early in the morning I walked through the wood for the last time. I had not said good-bye to anyone.

At the small station something peculiar happened. I was standing on the platform, my suitcase against my shins, my arms around my stuffed coat. The rails started to hum, and the stationmaster came out of his office. I knew him well, I had once made him a pair of pants. He walked up to me, asked where I was going; he saw the suitcase and wanted to bid me farewell. The strange thing was that I knew what I wanted to say but said nothing. The words whirled around in my head and could not escape. Shrugging his shoulders, he walked away. He did give a quick wave when the train left. I saw that his pants were too tight.

I thought for a long time about the words while I sat on the wooden folding seat on the platform between two railcars and saw the spruce forest pass me by. From the adjoining compartment I heard people talking to one another. I understood almost everything; I knew their words. That would become different, the American man had said, in the new land people spoke another language. How would I be able to know the names of things there? Would I have to relinquish an old name for every new one?

In the big station of Warsaw, we, the emigrants, were gathered and herded together on a remote platform. We were allowed to go into the city; the train would not depart until the evening, but I remained sitting on my suitcase and listened to all the Polish words that sounded through the station noises.

The trip took a long time; I got confused about the dates. Sometimes the train continued riding at night, sometimes all the emigrants had to get out in order to spend the night in a large barracks. Strange words came into my head; we rode through Germany. I had decided not to wash myself; then I wouldn't have to take off my coat. The bread that I had taken with me was finished, but that didn't matter, I was not hungry. There were so many emigrants! Mothers with children, young men with the tools of their trade on their backs, men from Russia, Poland, Germany. A friendly woman offered me something, it looked like a paprika pepper. Carefully, I shook my head no. I didn't want to open my mouth; I had to preserve the words of my old language as safely as possible. I dozed off and slept.

Rotterdam! I woke up with a start when the train braked abruptly and came to a halt. Around me emigrants were shouting and were pushing their suitcases out through the windows. The woman with the paprika wiped her children's faces clean with a handkerchief that she had first spit into. I didn't get up until everyone had left the carriage. There was creaking in my joints, and I got so dizzy that I had to grab hold of the luggage rack.

Rotterdam is hell. People bump up against you, want to go right through you, and bellow incomprehensible, loud words into your ears. When we filed out of the station the sunlight hit my face. They took us to the water where the light was even more glaring. And everywhere rowboats, coils of rope, carts, sailors, milkmaids, people!

In the immense, overcrowded night quarters I looked for a wooden plank against the back wall, far away from the windows. Eyes shut. Why can't a person close off his ears? I felt how my carefully preserved words were assailed first by the travelers and then by the piercing language of the inhabitants of Rotterdam. I stuffed my thumbs in my ears and hid my head in my coat.

The next morning the water started to speak to me. With their bundles and boxes the travelers stood on the round blue stones of the wharf. They had eaten breakfast at long tables in the middle of the hall. Deafening. I had gone to the end of the line when they were led out of the building. I tried to walk erect; I was going to a better life. At first I was happy to be in the open air. We had to wait. In the distance lay a large boat. Small, brisk waves splashed against the embankment. I listened; it sounded like children's giggling; what were they laughing at?...herring, bacon...They were laughing at me! Now I could understand it:

Mendel Bronstein is a miser
Buys no herring, eats no bacon,
None the wiser!

I rushed to the side, suddenly furious, and spit into the water. The paprika woman saw me and tugged at my coat. "You're attracting attention. You'd better stay in line," she said. I tried to look at the houses and no longer deigned to look at the water. Behind my back there was still laughter.

The crossing lasted almost two weeks, it was said. No one wanted to lie next to me because I stank. After a few days everyone stank. Still I ate nothing. Sometimes the woman brought me a mug of water. A greeting from the sea, I thought, watch out! I heard it batter the side of the ship; it shook me day and night. That was the large, threatening sound. Inside were the small sounds: a crying baby, snoring like creaking wood, and songs that tried to drive the poor words from my head. I cursed my ears. One night I carefully picked the largest darning needle from the case and pierced my eardrums. I screamed for a moment, but I felt it more than I could hear it.

Every morning the cleaning crew came to hose down the steerage. They pushed me to the side; with water they drove me against the wall, behind which was the water waiting for me. I felt it vibrate against my body. "Helga, Helga," said the water. Nothing to do with it. I had to be sure that I would reach the shore. In America, far inland, I would find a spruce forest, and there I would settle as a deaf tailor.

Ever since my ears were destroyed I slept well. When I lay awake, new worries came to me. Daily I thought of all my words in order not to lose them, but they seemed to be ever fewer in number. Helga had worn wooden things on her feet when she was cleaning the windows, I thought the next day. But what were those things called? Words were actively leaving me! They crawled out of my head, probably through my hair. When everyone was asleep, I took my scissors and cut it all of, as close as possible to my skin. Traitor! Under the mattress with it!

The woman was shocked when she saw me. She made knots in the corners of her handkerchief and put it on my head like a cap. She was wearing a beautiful dress, of chintz, and her children were wearing real shoes. Everyone was washing and cleaning themselves.

Suitcases were packed and closed. The heavy seas quieted down. We approached land.

Where they took us was a palace. From the packed outside deck you could see it on a small island. Red bricks, arched windows, glass-domed roofs that sparkled in the sun. We thronged in through a covered hall. They were going to kill us. Don't let on, otherwise the other people will be frightened. Or should I warn the woman? She thought that she was going to her husband and didn't know that she would soon be slaughtered. Very slyly I tried to pull the scissors from the case. Whatever window I looked through, I saw water.

No, they didn't kill me. A man with enormous feet, in a white coat, wanted to unbutton my collar. In disgust he looked at the streams of blood and pus that ran along my neck. He took a tailor's chalk and drew a cross on my coat. Someone took me away to a room upstairs. They tied me down to a plank, pulled the handkerchief from my head, and found the case in my inside pocket. I was disarmed.

I must have fainted; when I came to I felt the ground move. I felt at my side: iron bars. I looked: a round window, behind it the sea. I had lost.

I don't remember much about the journey back. I was still afraid of the water, but at the same time I had the exciting idea that Helga was there. When I closed my eyes, it seemed as if she spoke to me through the waves. She said that she was waiting for me. That was all. I did nothing.

On the gate of the new palace it said MAASOORD. It was on the water, but I no longer minded. They undressed me completely there and placed me in a bathtub. I screamed out, but after that I was quiet; I trusted the water and that was good. Later I got a needle in my arm through which they forced water into my body. After a week I could stand and they pulled out the needle. With wide open, moving mouths they stood in front of me, alternately pointing to the window and the soup pan on the table. I was allowed to go into the garden. Provided that I ate...

There was only one place I wanted to go. I started eating. Every day I sat in the garden, against the wall, behind which was the river.

Helga called me on a sunny, windy afternoon. The nurses were eating, the garden was empty. With my regained strength I climbed onto the bench, wrestled myself over the wall—the upright bits of broken glass reminded me of pricking spruce branches. There she is; I throw myself into her gray-green apron, I disappear in her cool embrace.

III. and IV.
Cato and Leendert

I

Rotterdam, May 1940

I sat in the kitchen and ate bread porridge. I was not hungry; my throat seemed closed.

When I placed the bowl, the soup bowl with the flower decorations, on the table, I trembled so violently that the milk spilled over the edge.

I was not hungry but I had to eat.

The sun shone on the window and made the oilcloth on the table glisten. It had never been so quiet here. I sat in Father's place, with my back to the light. My shadow fell over the porridge plate.

Fraud, I thought, fibber.

War had started. Father and Mother had fled to the polder and lodged temporarily with Aunt Alie. I sat at the table alone and ate my bread porridge.

The city teemed with fearful expectations; my own thoughts made me tremble. Say it!

No one could see me, and yet I blushed over my plate. I had

lied, and because it was war, and because it was Pentecost my cheeks were the color of flames. It was worse than the most cowardly treason.

You bring old bread to boil with some milk; the bread falls apart; it combines with the milk into a white, slimy mush. Sugar on top. A pat of butter, sunny trails of fat, nourishing. Sweet.

"The Missus needs me, father. I can't come with you."

"I have to put the holiday roast in the oven for her, mother; the Missus is counting on me."

I had sat down at the table with the *Hague Cookbook* and studied how to cook a large roast in the oven. I thought of Leendert.

The war had broken out; the Germans were in Overschie, in south Rotterdam, near the bridges. And I thought of Leendert. Of course I wouldn't go to my Missus—no use going there! I was free. He would visit me in the empty house. For a moment I would stand still on the landing as if paralyzed when the bell rang—then I'd pull on the rope and the door would fly open. He dashes up the stairs; I see the top of his head, hear his shoes graze the steps; he embraces me; I smell his lion odor.

I rinsed the cold porridge down the drain. Where was he? The sun was gone; it was dark in the kitchen. He should be here; he's off duty by now. Was he walking out of the gates of the Blijdorp zoo with big steps, was he waiting impatiently for the tram, did he decide to come here running?

I heard airplanes buzz the city today. Explosions, sirens, cars tearing through the streets. But I didn't hear the doorbell.

Pentecost Monday. I don't understand it. He has forgotten me. He has chosen the war; he has refused to close his eyes and ears to the bombing threat; he could not hold on to the longing for our own Pentecost celebration. I'm waiting in the kitchen; for me the war does not exist. I'm a twenty-four-year-old woman waiting for her lover. I'm not afraid of a bomb hit, not afraid of the conflagration, not afraid of the collapsing kitchen walls. I'm afraid that he has forgotten me.

I thought: you must listen to the radio, you must ask the neighbors if there is any news, you must visit Koba to see if she is afraid. But I didn't want to let the war in, and so I sat petrified on the kitchen chair.

I thought: you must be a caretaker of the house, a daughter for your parents, a support for your friend—but I was a woman who waited for her lover who didn't come. There is no war; there is a chance to be together for days and nights in an empty house. Come, leave your lions alone, rush through the strange city, come!

I put on my last dress. The mirror says that he is coming. My upper arms stick out of the dark blue billowing sleeves, so soft, so plump that he can't stay away any longer.

* * *

If I were still with the zebras, they would have called me up for sure. Then I'd be wearing a helmet now, would be lying under the Willems Road Bridge with my knapsack, would have pissed in my army pants out of fear.

You're a coward if you don't fight. General Winkelman needs everyone against the enemy, meaning everyone between twenty and fifty. Men. That means me. I turned twenty-five. I would be a good soldier.

The director would have none of it. I had to hand in my call-up card to him, and he took care of the rest. I think that he cheated, for only the predator keepers were exempted, and I was still working in the zebra meadow. Perhaps he already saw a lion tamer in me. He has an eye for that. The zoo is everything to him. He makes rounds every day; first he greets the animals and then us.

Today he looked pale. He wanted to speak with us in the feeding kitchen—so that the animals wouldn't hear it, I thought.

If the shooting continued, he said…

If more bombs were going to fall, he said…

If the fire continued raging, he said…

Then we would have to kill the animals. Lions, panthers, tigers in cages, surrounded by flames—that's impossible, that's a torture that he, the director, did not want to have on his conscience.

Release them, I thought, how wonderful it would be to finally set our animals free, to see how they would cleverly and regally lead themselves to safety along the shores of the Maas river, in the polder, in the Kralingen Wood.

Releasing them would be irresponsible, he said somberly. It would be all right for the hoofed animals, the monkeys, the birds. Not for the predators.

I'll bring you a weapon, he said, when it's time. He looked at the head zookeeper: "You have to do it, Borst. I'm counting on you. It's the only way."

I went to clean the inside cage. Outside on his terrace, Alexander was on patrol: five meters one way and five meters back. I heard his rump crash against the side walls when he turned. He felt our agitation and tried to calm himself by walking back and forth. After I cleaned the floor, I spread a bed of fresh hay for him.

I prefer not to recount how we heard explosions and bomb hits all afternoon. In the feeding kitchen, deep inside the building, the racket wasn't too bad. Borst was sitting motionless, deep in thought, on an upside-down bucket. He was waiting.

Alexander roared on the terrace. He was afraid; he imagined himself in Africa and saw the savanna burning. I opened the hatch and he squeezed into the inside cage, his familiar night-quarters.

If the fire continues…

If the bombs keep falling…

Then the director came in. He carried a package under his arm. His lips trembled under his mustache. That it was time. That it had to be done now. Colonel Scharroo had moved his headquarters; there would be no end to the hostilities; the negotiations had failed; we had to take into account the continuation of the bombing; things would become much worse; the Germans had no mercy.

He placed the package on the table.

I kept apart when he instructed Borst. At the top vertebra of the neck and then slanting upward, into the skull. Every animal in its own cage, to prevent panic. First give them plenty to eat. I didn't want to hear it. Borst was nodding, caressing the pistol absent-mindedly.

The director walked away, downcast, with empty hands. He was destroying his own garden; he ordered his pride and joy to be shot to pieces. Capitulation. I experienced the bitter taste of disdain. I felt the quickened heartbeat of resistance.

None of us went home that night. We kept watch; we waited for the execution of the animals. I dozed off on the stock of hay; right before I nodded off I saw Cato sitting on the embankment of Kralingen Pond, her hands hidden in her muff, her pale face encircled by the dark cap. Her eyes. I sped up, I heard my skates scratching the black ice.

* * *

There was screaming in the street; I woke with a start. I had fallen asleep with my head on my arms at the kitchen table. Sugar grains pricked my skin; my back hurt. Something had come into my head that was not good; it was so big that I no longer felt myself. I pressed my nails into my arms; there were red half moons in my skin, but I didn't feel it. I felt like banging my face against the granite kitchen counter but instead wandered down the stairs, away, outside.

"You have to go to confession," said Koba, "and everything will be forgiven." I was so happy to see her, I clung to her skinny shoulders and for a moment I cried against her apron. I had told her everything about Leendert. Everything. She had shaken her head in disapproval: first get engaged, then marry. And the rest not until afterward. That's how she thought, and that is why she wanted me to confess my plans, my sins. We stood in the small front yard. Wet sheets fluttered around us; it was as if we were walking through a hall with moving white walls. I looked at Koba's chapped, red hands; I picked up the empty laundry basket and followed her into the scullery where it smelled of soup.

Suddenly I felt sick, weak. There was black. Falling.

When I came to, I was lying in Koba's room on the guest bed. My shoes stood next to the wall. The door was slightly ajar, and from downstairs came unintelligible snatches of conversation. Someone coughed. I've always hated twilight. It's awful that the day is ending.

The floor creaked when I got up, and the voices downstairs fell silent. There was a small, closed window through which I looked at the evening. The sheets floated above the grass like angels' wings. At the horizon there was a line of fire that I didn't understand.

Downstairs Koba's parents were sitting at the table, and it made me think right away of Father and Mother far away in the polder, enjoying Aunt Alie's applesauce, unaware of what was happening here. Koba's father is a ticket collector on the tram. His uniform had been tossed on a chair. How it looked in the city, he said, we couldn't even imagine. The trams were no longer running; the carriages stood abandoned on the rails. Broken glass everywhere, there was still some in his shoe soles. Did he mean that someone had smashed the windows? A German soldier? He shook his head. Pressure waves. The intense blast of air smashed the glass. He had left his tram and had gone home. The oil refineries in Pernis were burning.

I wanted to ask how things were in the area near the zoo, but I didn't dare. We had to sit down; we ate soup; Koba's mother went on about the sheets that would become dirty from the soot settling on them.

Finally we were lying in bed; Koba's face was dimly visible in the dark against her pillow. How strange it is, I thought, to lie here in this narrow bed while outside the city crackles and smolders. How crushed I am by his absence. How empty it is between my arms.

Koba was crying. I slipped under the blanket with her and held her. Her fear was unfamiliar to me, her grief didn't touch me. She sobbed that the Germans would come if the bridges were not destroyed in time; I grieved about my Pentecost holidays, destroyed by Leendert who had not come. She feared the destruction of her house, her street, her city. I couldn't care less about that. He doesn't want me. It's over.

I caressed Koba's bony arms and thought about the blond hairs on Leendert's muscular wrists. I listened to Koba's sniffling and thought of Leendert's uneven breathing when he kissed me.

Tomorrow I'd go on my way; I'd go and look for him. I would walk in the direction of the animals, and at the end of my journey I would find him, my man, my beast.

* * *

The director betrayed his own zoo and Borst collaborated with him. That afternoon the animals received extra portions of feed to make them sluggish, lazy, and distracted. Afterward Borst went by the cages. There must have been a silencer on the weapon, for I heard only a dull report. Then a heavy animal body slipping onto the stone floor, then the rattling of the next cage door.

I would resist to the end if I were the boss here. I would never harm so much as a hair on one of my animals; I'd rather perish with them in the flames.

In the watering trough in front of Alexander's night cage, I was busy scrubbing the feeding trays and drinking bowls when Borst appeared in the doorway with his murder weapon. I rammed the iron trays with full force against the granite counter; Borst's voice was lost in the scraping of the stiff brushes against metal, in the roar of water on stone.

He took a step forward and with his free hand reached for the faucet. I looked up, I had to. I looked at him. The time had come.

"I'll do it myself," I said. I hadn't thought of it beforehand, but I heard myself say it and knew that it was good. Borst nodded, gave me the pistol, and showed me how it should be done.

"This is the last one. I'm going into the garden; we're opening all the cages. After that, all of you may go. Good luck." He turned around and walked away, fumbling for the big bunch of keys in his back pocket.

I went into the night cage where Alexander lay gnawing a rib of beef. He lifted his enormous head and waved it back and forth as a greeting. He had known me as long as he lived. I got him when he was young; he saw me as a mother, I thought. I was supposed to go and sit next to him, hit him on the shoulders, place the pistol in the dimple at the base of his head. And then. It had to be done; Borst was surely standing in the passageway, waiting for the shot. I would have to give the pistol back to him. I had to do something.

The recoil made it feel as though I had shot into my own arm. The crack had numbed my ears. I smelled smoldering hay. Nervously I stamped out the small fire that started. The barrel of the weapon was red-hot. Frightened, Alexander got up on his legs but lay down again at my whispered command. I leaned against the wall of the small trough, dizzied by my deed. What would happen next, I didn't know, but I had not capitulated—that was a fact.

Standing in the middle of the wide footpath to the monkey rock, Borst was giving directions. I handed over the pistol and gave a brief nod when he asked if it had been done. He gave me the keys to the hoofed animal quarters, and I went off through the twilit garden.

I took a deep breath and smelled the foul burning odor, saw the smoke columns in the distance. Not until then.

Suddenly I remembered that at this moment she was waiting for me in her parents' house, the empty house. I hoped that she had gone away, to a friend or a neighbor. That she understood that I had other things to do. That she was not afraid.

The hoofed animal quarters are built in a big circle. I walked around slowly and opened all the outside gates. The old zebra pair recognized me. I lured the stallion with a lump of sugar that he kissed from my flat hand. Tears welled in my eyes at the touch of those soft zebra lips. I opened the gate wide, but the animals didn't understand and remained standing calmly behind the bars.

Evening fell. One by one the keepers trudged away from the grounds, superfluous now that the animals had been released. They wanted to go to their homes; they wanted to hear what tomorrow would bring; they wanted to be near their families to wait for the fighting or the capitulation. I raised my hand, mumbled a greeting, and kept walking. The monkeys had also remained in their cages. Only the birds had made use of their freedom; I heard them scratching and scraping in the trees.

The large entrance to the zoo stood open. Everyone could walk in and out. We no longer existed.

I slept near Alexander, man and lion. In the morning I gave him fresh water and a leftover cow's leg. The sun was shining. I rolled up my sleeves and sat daydreaming on the steps. Before the first airplanes were visible, Alexander roared unrestrained in his inside cage. A rain of bombs, a sea of fire, anti-aircraft guns. I smiled. Winkelman had not buckled; he preferred to sacrifice the city rather than capitulate. Protected by the concrete wall of the predatory-animal house, I kept watching how the airplanes in formation headed for the center and dropped their loads like birds shitting in flight.

I felt nothing but a vague satisfaction.

* * *

Here I go in the dress with the beautiful sleeves, the dress that I won't take off until I find Leendert. I walk through the still quiet street; Koba slips her arm through mine; she doesn't leave me alone. Oh, now it's warm; now the sun warms my bare arms; now I can breathe and silence the reproaches inside me. That I misled my parents, that I coaxed my frightened friend out into the street against her will—none of it counts. I'm going to Leendert.

Houses are in ruins at the other side of the water. We see helmeted German soldiers in an open car. The sun sparkles and shimmers on the constantly moving water. The light is limber. A day for sailing, for rowing a boat together through the reeds.

So many people on the street. They speak to us, something terrible is going to happen, we have to flee, to take cover, to bury ourselves. Koba listens and trembles; I turn away—I still have far to walk.

"You have to go to confession," Koba says again. "You've done things that are wrong. God will punish us."

She points up, where not a cloud can be seen in the clear sky. Suddenly a splitting wail breaks loose from hundreds of sirens. People start running; they push one another into houses and doorways. Koba tugs at my arm. I'm standing motionless in a whirlpool of speed and noise. Then the street, which a moment ago was full of life, is deserted. The sound of the sirens subsides, starts wailing again, and finally dies down.

In the silence I hear a vague drone that swells. From very far away, from the east, a swarm of airplanes is flying in our direction. Koba screams and starts pushing me to move. Surprised, I look at the sky; dark specks are falling from the machines. There are so many, and the engines throb so powerfully!

"To the church!" screams Koba. She drags me along; I follow without paying attention to anything. Then there is a woman who lets us in through a side door.

"To the vault," she says, "it's safe there; it won't collapse." She shows us a large safe with strong, steel walls. We lift out the silver bowls and candlesticks; they stand around us on the stone floor. One after the other we climb into the vault. Then the woman pulls the door shut.

I lie next to Koba, just like last night. We fold a Communion robe into a pillow; with our legs pulled up we lie listening to the muffled detonations of the bombs. Koba and the woman say prayers. I remain silent.

Avalanches of rubble crash down onto our safe vault. The church collapses. First we are stupefied with fear, then we get up and feel along the walls. They are still there.

Weak, we fall down; it seems as if the thin, tepid air is barely being sucked in. My head is spinning; I feel Koba lie next to me limply; I squeeze her arm, hard—nothing happens.

Suddenly I want out. I have to go to Leendert; I have to know if he's alive. I have to wrest myself from this pitch-black space before I lose consciousness. With all my strength I push against the door, what I take to be a door. It doesn't give. I follow the wall with my hands. Past the corner I push again, and again, and again. All around I throw myself against the walls; I brace myself and press my shoulders against the wall of the vault. Blood is ringing in my ears, all my muscles tremble, but the vault doesn't open.

Then I shake my vault mates furiously by the shoulders; I kick their sides; I curse them out. They have to wake up so that I'm not here alone, here in this iron box where it is becoming increasingly hot. It strangles me; I've opened my eyes wide but I see nothing, I see nothing.

The city is burning, the church is ablaze, and the flames are licking the vault. Like the holiday roast in the oven. The cookbook. My own fault. Punishment.

The floor is ice-cold against my calves. The Kralingen Pond, frozen over. Look, there he comes, it's Leendert; he is skating toward me and we fall; we tumble onto the ice; it's so cold, but he embraces me; he presses me so close to him that my heart stops; pushes his mouth against my throat finally, finally…

* * *

The last thing I do as zookeeper is to open the doors that lead to Alexander's cage. I greet my lion; he looks at me for a moment and then continues devouring the bone between his forepaws.

In rubber boots, in overalls, I walk into the city, dizzy with fatigue. Sometimes there is sun where I expect shade, then I realize that façades, blocks of houses, and whole streets are gone. Craters in the pavement, fire in the rubble, creaking of unstable walls.

The farther south I go, the faster I start walking. The greater my agitation, the more hurriedly I suck in the foul air. Burned coffee, smoldering tobacco, untold numbers of scorched objects. The street where Cato lives is unrecognizable, the windows of her house are black holes, framed by flames. The window panes lie in splinters in the street.

Onward. There is a man who is pulling a cart with a child in it. He gives me bread. I haven't eaten for days. His eyes sparkle. It's over, he says. Winkelman has announced the capitulation. Now we are occupied. I help him to pull the cart. We're going to the Kralingen Wood where there are no houses that can fall down on us—there is water, no fire.

I see our ostriches again on Coolsingel. They step elegantly between the embers, move their heads toward the ground, then pull back, frightened. I point with my hand, speechless; the man shakes his head, nods. We end up in a caravan of dismayed people, on our way to the pond. I stay with the man with the child; we're lying in a field; I smell the grass; I close my eyes. The war has been lost; I have lost the lion. My throat becomes dry with anger. I'm suddenly so furious that I have to get up, have to stamp on the green field and wildly lash out around me with my arms.

There, there across the street, she's sitting there!

She sits up, leaning on her elbows, she motions to me.

Then I run to my Cato; I trip over babies, pans with food, and baby carriages; at the edge of the pond I slip in the mud; I fall; I plunge backward and the rusty rail of the broken gate penetrates my skull, spears me to the earth through my first cervical vertebra, like a pin on a military map.

v. The Doctor

I should have killed him.

They banged against the door of the operating room, and I was annoyed. I didn't look up. I was closing a compound leg fracture and was bent over the long row of sutures. A surgeon has to train himself not to react directly, physically, to distractions. The annoyance should not affect the way you move; imagine making a sudden movement that causes the knife to slip!

When I operate, shock and irritation don't go farther than my head. That's bad enough. I heard the stomping of heavy shoes in the hall, someone barked a command in German, and the wheels of a stretcher squeaked. I remained seated, bent over my sutures. I didn't look up. Softly but insistently I said: "Not here. O.R. two."

I could have killed him. In a depressed fracture you compare the depth of the wound to the thickness of the exposed skull. When I examined the exposed skull, I could have pressed deep into the gray mass. Continue pushing into the brainstem—one lever action and the vital functions will be destroyed. Breathing, for example. No one would notice except perhaps the head nurse. I would wait until she was distracted for a moment; she had to take care of the anesthesia, monitor the hoses and valves of the machine. Plenty of opportunity.

I should have killed him.

I saw my shoes sticking out from under the operating apron. I had never dared to go into the O.R. that dirty. Dust and grit were stuck to the red-brown bloodstains; a soiled trail of gauze had become wedged in the tread of my sole and dragged across the stone floor.

Three months before those fateful May days, I became the head of surgery at the hospital on Coolsingel. A three-hundred bed unit! I felt completely at home there. Action. Variety. Speed. When the Germans invaded I was of course horror-stricken, but I also caught myself feeling delighted—as if I were a boy again and a fire had broken out somewhere. You found it awful, but it was simply exciting.

War surgery! In spite of myself my heart leapt. I'm a professional. All those wounded, the pressure of triage, the dramatic working through the night—the hospital administration would immediately realize that my appointment had been a bull's-eye.

And that's how it went, the first days of the war. We worked ourselves into a sweat; we patched up all our patients as fast as possible and sent home those who could at least breathe on their own.

On May 14, I was eating lunch with the senior medical officer. The cafeteria is at the front of the building. Was at the front side. There is no building.

When the rumbling started, I ran back to the unit. We carried, wheeled, and pushed all the patients who were still there to the bicycle shed in the cellar. Anti-personnel bombs. Smoke and soot. It was pitch-dark in broad daylight. That causes panic. In me as well. I was standing on the staircase with a few patients and Karel, my assistant. One of the women couldn't stop screaming. That was my deliverance. Hysteria, I thought, an attack of hysteria that I have to stop. Then I was a doctor again and became calm.

The bombardment lasted an eternity, fifteen minutes. After that it was quiet. Through the cracked hall window, I saw that the fire brigade was rolling out hoses. They remained slack. There was no water. I ordered Karel to evacuate the patients to the Catholic church in Van Oldenbarneveldstraat. As a surgeon you have to be able to make quick decisions.

"Climb onto the pulpit when they're inside," I said. "Address them. Keep up the morale." He looked at me surprised and went into the basement.

I left the blazing hospital. I had escaped death and was bursting with a drive for action. Through destroyed streets, past burning houses, I ran to Bergweg Hospital, without looking around. The Germans had caused me to lose everything, but I didn't acknowledge defeat.

The dead lay on the lawn between the pavilions. Housewives, workers, children. I stormed in. In the halls I made my way to the ward on a narrow path left between two rows of moaning, screaming people.

My surgical colleague there was an older man. I encountered him in the ward, where he pottered about in a stupor with a small bottle of Mercurochrome in his hands.

"Is my house still standing?" he asked. "Have you seen my house?"

With his little bottle he was standing among people with legs torn off, and he was thinking about his house! I asked if he had sufficient morphine for the hopeless cases, and how many O.Rs he had ready.

"What do you want to do here?" he asked, surprised.

"Operate, of course. Save what can be saved. And right away."

The head nurse came and stood next to us. A reliable, solid woman with an immaculate white cap on her graying hair.

"I think that I'll go and check on my house after all," said my colleague. I was baffled.

"Then you'll transfer control here to me," I said. "That is the condition. Otherwise I'll lodge a complaint against you." He nodded, placed the bottle of Mercurochrome on a nightstand, and shuffled out of the ward.

"Pins," I said to the nurse. "Pen and paper. We're making thorough rounds. I'll examine, you'll write the diagnosis and degree of urgency on a note and pin it to the patient."

She was standing ready. She had ordered a second O.R. to be ready so that we could work while the other room was being cleaned. Panting, the pharmacist came upstairs with his total morphine supply.

What bombs can do to a human body cannot be described. Grimly determined, I hurried through the halls. Sometimes I couldn't do anything but give a morphine injection, then a gentle death was the best thing attainable. Gradually my hatred for the perpetrators of this inferno grew until I trembled with fury. But I had to do my work. There was a child, a little boy. A ripped open stomach, a shell fragment deep in his small skull, and shallow, quick breathing. Impossible to save, but conscious. He screamed for his mother.

"She's already lying outside," said the head nurse. I ordered a nurse to go outside with scissors. "Cut off a piece of her dress, quickly!"

She came back running with a green piece of cloth in her hand, part of a summer dress with flowers. I placed the cloth against the child's cheek and filled the syringe.

We were short of needles. Usually the night porter would be sharpening needles, but in the chaos of the war days, that didn't happen. Rather than using blunt needles, I ran the few sharp ones we had through alcohol time after time.

The O.R. seemed an oasis of quiet. Until those German medical orderlies, the Sanitäter, forced their way in. Two of them pushed the squeaking gurney through the swing doors. From the corner of my eye I saw a man in uniform lying down, his cap between his feet. It confused me for a moment. A two-headed monster.

I was bent over that leg fracture. Almost finished. During the suturing I thought of the screaming child that we had quieted down with his mother's dress. Undoubtedly dead by now.

They screamed at us, in German. Where was the Director, they were bringing a very high ranking, seriously wounded patient who had to be treated now, immediately, by the best surgeon. I understand German and speak it too, but I kept quiet. I placed the last suture and looked up.

"This is General Student," said one of the soldiers. He looked at me and his eyes narrowed. "The General will not be treated by a black man. Where is the senior medical officer?"

Silence. I couldn't manage to say anything. The nursing supervisor came to roll away the leg fracture. Embarrassed, she remained standing behind the Germans. We heard General Student breathe with difficulty.

"Here is the best surgeon in Rotterdam." The clear voice of the head nurse. She also added that we did not appreciate insults, and that the doctor—meaning I—might possibly be inclined to examine the General provided that the escorts would withdraw to the hall.

Then I recovered my voice. "O.R. two," I managed to say. It sounded strangely hoarse.

The nursing supervisor went ahead of the Germans; the stretcher disappeared. I looked at the head nurse, expected a knowing glance, perhaps a wink, but her face was serious and inaccessible.

My skin is dark. Darker than that of the others. I've seldom had cause to think about it. In elementary school we sang "Moriaantje, black as soot." Snickering, a girl pointed at me. The teacher reprimanded her. When those Germans called me "black," I didn't even think of myself at first. At my academic high school, in the student organization, during my medical training—no one ever called me names. I feel I'm just like the others. I walk in the street in a tailor-made suit, I'm a surgeon. Chief of surgery. My father was a prominent ship owner; my mother is descended from a patrician family from Rotterdam. Perhaps there were overseas adventures, an ancestor from Surinam or the East Indies who passed on his hereditary matter under a white cover until it was expressed in me? I am a citizen of Rotterdam.

I walked to the other O.R. The general was already lying on the table; the stretcher with the cap on it was standing in a corner. "Out!" I said to the soldiers. "You are a source of germs. It's against regulations. Out."

They remained standing near the operating table and followed our actions carefully, with pistols drawn. Out of annoyance I didn't take a clean apron. I started work in work clothes that were stained with blood and bone marrow and even threw my operating cap on the floor. I sweated.

The head nurse had cut open the uniform jacket; we could simply pull the shreds from the body. I inspected the cranial trauma while one of the Germans recounted the circumstances. Capitulation negotiations in Headquarters, with the mayor—a stray bomb hit the house and a beam crashed down on the skull of the general.

Depressed fractures are exceptionally nasty. The skull is supposed to remain closed. The brains are meticulously packed in membranes, fluid, and bone. This treasury is not meant to be penetrated. The very idea makes people nauseated. Fearful. Confused.

An infant has immature cranial plates, and on the top of the head the fontanel pulsates. If you put your finger on that weak spot, you feel the mobility, the vulnerability of what lives inside it. Many parents find that unpleasant. A knitting needle would slide in without encountering resistance.

The skull of the general was deeply dented on the left side. I observed a good-sized laceration of the scalp, a dirty wound with wooden splinters and bits of soot inside it. Bone fragments stuck up from the lesion and a grayish brain mass welled up between the edges of the wound.

"Ringer's!" I said to the nurse. She gave me the bottle before I had finished speaking. Carefully I started to wash away the brain tissue. I cleaned the wound and removed wood splinters with tweezers. It looked hopeless.

"Probe." I was handed the glass rod and lowered it into the wound past the broken cranial plate. Two centimeters. I stood perfectly still.

In the brain that I touched, the destruction of my city had

been plotted. These brains were responsible for that garden downstairs filled with the dead, for those needlessly wrecked bodies in the halls, for the uncontrolled screaming that vaguely penetrated the operating room. This man had destroyed my hospital, occupied my city, requisitioned my country.

"Start the anesthesia?" asked the head nurse. Her voice rang through the space. I relaxed my shoulders. I was a doctor. City Doctor. It was my duty to heal where I could, without regard to the person. Those Germans who were glancing at us with revolvers at the ready might consider me a black ape—I would show them what civilization was.

I did a lumbar puncture without any anesthesia, although the general was still conscious. He didn't say a word, but his eyes followed our movements. Hardly any spinal fluid pressure. Bloody liquid in the test tube. The nurse administered the liberating ether and I went to work. I removed the shattered bone and sewed up the cerebral membranes as best I could. Finally I pulled the scalp over the artificial fontanel and closed the wound. Although I had put in a drain, I was practically sure that a blockage would occur, with loss of consciousness and epileptic seizures as a result. I had to give Phenobarbital preventively, even though our supply was almost exhausted.

We didn't look at the Germans when we left the O.R. In the hall stood the nursing supervisor with two cups of soup. I felt lightheaded, as if I were acting in a bewildering dream.

During ward rounds, the following days, I kept having to conquer a certain aversion when I got to the bed of the general. That man had all the luck in the world—no infections, no complications, and a gradual return of his functions. His speech was still defective for the time being; he could say only one sentence, and he did that as soon as he caught sight of me: "*Sie haben mir das Leben gerettet!*" He repeated those words, "you saved my life," as long as he saw me. Now that he was recovering, a cranioplasty would have to be done. Not by me, I decided. Let him find a German doctor.

The practice of my own shattered and burned hospital was continued on hospital ships in the harbor. There, on a sunny day, a company of German soldiers appeared and entered the operating room uninvited. General Student wanted to thank me before he left for another front. He shook my hand for a long time. "*Sie haben mir das Leben gerettet*," he said again. He did not have an unkind face. I was silent.

Occupation. Curfew. Racial laws. I worked.

One evening, when I came off the ship, a woman was waiting for me on the wharf. She had tied a dark blue scarf over her hair. I didn't recognize her; not until she started to speak did I know who she was. The head nurse of the Bergweg Hospital.

She helped me. I didn't want it, of course not. I didn't see myself as the representative of an inferior race, but the occupier thought differently. She found me a hiding place, and I let myself be convinced. I had no choice. Armed with cyanide capsules I headed for uselessness. Being betrayed was a relief.

Transport. I would like to snarl at the guards that I had saved their General's life, that I was not a negro but a City Doctor. I sat on the drafty planks of the freight car and knew with great clarity that none of it made any difference. I should have killed him. The Germans would have shot me dead on the spot, but I would have avenged the destruction of my city.

Now! I bit through the cyanide capsule and felt the poison burn in my mucous membranes. To act, even acting out of despair, is better than waiting passively.

In my last thoughts I saw myself press the probe forcefully into the General's brain.

I should have killed him.

VI. …and I am Sara

The stage is dark. Sara's face is lit. She stands on the side and speaks directly to the audience.

The year was so dark. I had thought that everything would be light. Exams passed, success, spotlights. For a whole year I had slaved away at complicated theories about Couperus. And then wrote it up nicely. It turned into a work that I was proud of. On the day of graduation I was completely overcome by nervousness, for I was going to be questioned for a whole hour. When I entered the department and saw my name in neon letters on the immense board, I started to get in the mood. It was a play and I was the star. I could take my time, elaborate, make jokes, and I managed to do just that. I was extremely focused; I listened to the shuffling in the hall, heard my parents and friends chatter and giggle together, but didn't lose the thread of my argument for a moment.

After that there was the waiting. And then all of us cramming into that room. An eight! I signed my name and then stood up to give a speech myself. For my thesis advisor, to whom I'd gone every week for advice as if he were my therapist. "Usually it isn't until after you're dead that they tell you how well you've done things," I said, "but I want to tell you now." He blushed red as a beet and his eyes glistened.

It was a festive week. The next day Peter graduated. Luckily I was first. He's my little brother, but he's better at everything. At least in matters of study and discipline. I'm very proud of him and also jealous. Sometimes.

We had a dinner at our family's favorite restaurant. Flowers, presents, and speeches that made everyone cry.

Later there was an enormous party for all of Pete's and my friends. *Style your hair funky or cool 'cause both of us are done with school!* we wrote on the invitation under a photo of both of us singing and totally smashed. Together we're strong, we're a unit and always help each other. From all the places where I had ever worked came delegates wearing wigs and with glitter in their hair. Maria wore a silver wig and I a black one.

Then suddenly it was autumn, and it started to rain. All of them had jobs, those friends of mine. Peter too. He wore a pinstriped suit. Nice, fascinating jobs; they earned a lot of money and met interesting people. They did what they wanted to do and were successful at it. I was short on money and went to the temp agency for ten dollars per hour. I dreamed of singing on television and of becoming world-famous. My vocal cords had been declared unfit. Too short, or too stiff, or something. It would be all right just for fun, said the stupid bitch of a doctor, but not professionally. I was hoarse and croaky. Had started to smoke again, and drink. Because of stress.

Instead, try and become a journalist. With that thesis I had certainly shown that I could remain seated at a desk. I signed up for a prestigious course and was accepted by a klutz with bad hair who told me that it was very demanding and difficult.

We had to write articles that were ripped to pieces every Saturday. Then we had to write them again. "Positive" criticism! I ground my teeth. At home I had placed six stacks of research papers for each article on the floor. Against the door I pasted a big planning board on which I charted my progress. I was going to see it through. "It doesn't always have to be nice," said Mom. She thought that everything I wrote was wonderful. Because she's my mother. That didn't help me at all.

"You've always given me the illusion that life is great," I said to her. "I was always happy, and so were you. You lied. It's not great at all, it's terrible. A struggle. Everything becomes a mess right away; there is no way to organize and control it. You never prepared me for that."

Then she'd go and replenish my bank balance and pay my bills. But that's not what I meant.

I want to be an adult and be able to do things myself. Open my mail on time and put it in stacks. Have money left at the end of the month. Be able to be alone. Not always worry if others like me. Trust that I can do it. Stop longing for those bygone Wednesday afternoons when Mom would pick us up from school and we'd go to see the bird spider in the Artis zoo or steal tiny bananas in the Hortus botanical garden. When we sang songs at the piano. And life was like that.

I struggled through the autumn and through a dreadful spring. I worked on my C.V., sent solicitation letters to television stations and art organizations. All of them pledged to keep my letter just in case, thank you very much. No positions right now. In the bottom of the drawer. "Hang in there," said Mom, "it doesn't always work right away, chin up." I hate spring, when everyone is having fun except for me.

All my girlfriends had boyfriends. That's not true, but still. Peter had Boukje. And his great job. He was living on the floor above me. It will be endless discussions and singing songs like we used to do in our bedroom at home, I had thought. But he didn't return until late in the evening in his power suit, and all weekend long he stayed in bed with Boukje.

When I'm so down I do stupid things. I drank too much and got involved with a boy in the café on the corner. He turned out to be a creep, crazy; he thought that he had power over me, that I belonged to him. He walked past my house and put strange notes in my mailbox. Rang the bell. Just stood there. I became afraid. Not just afraid, but in a panic. Dad came to get me and I crawled onto Mom's lap. I would have liked nothing better than her mashing a banana and a rusk to feed me like a baby. I slept upstairs, next to my parents' bed. And I had already turned twenty-seven.

That birthday was awful. I didn't want to eat in the city but simply at home. Mom had made something elaborate, I don't remember what. I felt so wretched that I couldn't eat. A dessert of course, a strawberry tart. They had bought a stack of presents for me to cheer me up. At least fifteen packages, in Saint Nicholas wrapping paper. I had to cry and stormed upstairs, to my old room. There's been nothing but old junk in it since I left home. Doesn't make you cheery either. Dad took us back to the city, stony-faced. Silence in the car. Later I got into an argument with Pete. "You can't behave like that," he said, "they do their best to make things nice for you, and you ruin it."

Shit, I thought. It isn't nice. It's easy for him to say with his girlfriend and his work and his accounts in order. I sit here surrounded by unopened bills and rejection letters and I'm alone. No one understands how I really feel. They think that everything is OK, that I'm happy. Hang in there, they say.

Yet it bothered me; I was sorry for Mom and Dad. I called them the next day. I was sitting on a terrace chatting with a friend and suddenly felt very selfish and childish. I got Dad on the telephone. "It doesn't matter," he said, "you're still our sweetie."

Everything has to change, I thought. I'm going to take my life in hand. To organize myself, I bought beautiful colored folders. On them I pasted labels: *home, work, insurance, me*. That was project number one.

Project number two: Be nice to the cactus. It was in my house when I started living there, left behind by the previous tenants. Brownish, half rotted, bulging out of its filthy pot. If you tried to take care of it, it left nasty spines in your fingers that were impossible to get out. I had put it on the balcony behind a screen. Now I was going to repot it, wearing garden gloves that I had bought for the occasion. All the pieces that dropped off in the process I put in separate pots. They were allowed to be inside, on saucers, in a row.

Project three was the gym. Every day, work on the body for an hour. Even if my neighbor Heleen didn't come along. I'd get, and keep, firm buttocks.

I was going to carry out my three projects. Summer was coming.

The lights are turned off and are turned back on in the living room scene: a sofa with pillows, a coffee table with a stack of Privé *magazines and newspapers, a kitchen with a refrigerator on one side, a wardrobe on the other side.*

Soft light. Doors opening to the garden—with fruit trees. During the performance it becomes increasingly dark outside.

Sara enters wearing bicycle shorts and a top, her hair tied up with a rubber band. She pushes the racing bike into the room and puts it behind the sofa. Takes off her backpack, pulls out her cell phone and places it on the table. Kicks off her shoes. The cell phone rings; she answers.

—Sara?
—Hi! No, at home. At my parents', but they aren't here. On vacation. Pete also.
—Biked along the water. Very nice. I'm going to rest now. Wonderful that those Spanish guests have gone!
—Eat? No, I'm dead. I'd have to go into the city. And early tomorrow morning I have to go back to that rotten job. I prefer sleeping here. You don't mind, do you?
—[Laughs] Cheer up! I'll see you tomorrow.

Takes enormous jogging pants from the closet, puts them on, dances through the room, takes a cold drink from the refrigerator, and sprawls on the sofa.

Oh, that office. Day in, day out. But tomorrow is Friday, and I'll let it all hang out!!

I see only my computer screen. And the work cafeteria. This afternoon we were sitting there with croquettes for lunch. One of my thousands of colleagues was telling us that he sells a line of personal care products to his friends at Tupperware-like parties. All the people at our table became enthusiastic: What kind of products are they? How much do you earn with that?

I can't believe my eyes. They buy sunglasses with lollipop holders. I don't understand their jokes. Recently we had a company outing in a resort for senior citizens. We played bonding games, lifted one another through nets and did jigsaw puzzles without talking. Fortunately I escaped with a colleague who really is very nice. There was a tandem race, and we got lost accidentally on purpose. We managed to sit and enjoy a cigarette and talk in the forest.

In the evening they served us some steak that had been fried in the afternoon. Just reheat at six o'clock—these bureaucrats will eat anything.

I write about disability insurance, collective employment contracts, the Euro, and the health and safety law. Mostly I surf the internet or email, which is not allowed. "It's alarmingly quiet. Where is everyone? I'm at work right now. On a red chair. Straight in front of me I see a screen with more and more letters. Behind it a tall plant. Well, here I am. And I am Sara."

Grrr!

My head is filled with at least a hundred plans and resolutions. Call or email all my friends. Make a date with each of them at least once every two weeks. Learn to play bridge, for bridge can be an answer but will also give an answer. Play Yahtzee more often. Cook new dishes and write them down in a recipe book. Lunch with Dad. Take care of my nails. Go to the movies with Mom. To the Concertgebouw. To the Melkweg club. To Paradiso. Rent videos with Kevin. Read a good book. Go to the opera. Organize my clothes. Go to the dentist, in time. Learn to brake when skateboarding.

If I could steer all that energy in one direction, if I could bundle it—perhaps I could still become a singer. Control my vocal cords with pure willpower. Then what I want will be the same as what I can do.

Cries; blows her nose.

Oh yes, a music stand.

Gets up, rummages around in the closet and takes out a folded music stand. Holds it up triumphantly.

In the front of the orchestra. A real orchestra. Second oboe. The man next to me, the first oboe, said: "You don't have your own music stand? Not very professional!"

Fathead. I am taking oboe lessons again, fortunately. Just as before, except that now I want to know exactly what I'm doing. I used to just play. It's not singing, but it resembles it. You have to hold back. All that air that wants to escape. Hold on to it. Control.

Before going on vacation, I took my oboe home, and my old music pieces. Marcello, Cimarosa. Then I played with Mom. I couldn't keep it up for very long, but Dad said that my tone was already coming back. Mom was glad that I was going to play in the orchestra. "You'll love it," she said, "you lose yourself in the music and yet you soar above it on your oboe. And all those beautiful pieces!"

Of course she means that she thinks it's good that I'm letting go of that dream of singing and will do something that is possible. If you can't do it one way, do it another way; that's what she means. I understand it, but I don't say anything. She doesn't either; she knows better. She played beautifully around my melodic line. Playing together with her goes naturally, we never have to agree on anything beforehand. She's always willing. My Mother's Day present when I was eight or so was that she could play recorder duets with me all day long. She still talks about that.

Puts the music stand into her backpack. Opens the doors to the garden.

Really warm. Just like Italy. Such a wonderful vacation, so unexpected. I was planning to go, to visit my Italian friends, but I wanted to go with Kevin. It was still all right then—it was in the spring. Later we reached a point when I no longer understood our relationship at all. He didn't want to go on vacation with me, or perhaps he did, but then there couldn't be anything between us, or be separate and meet each other or not—it drove me crazy. Forget it, I thought, I'd rather no vacation.

Maria said: "Be finished with it! I'm taking off, we're going together." She had only a week. Yet it was wonderful. I had been there when I was fourteen; Mom gave me the map along with the old route marked on it. It gave me a well-traveled feeling.

Sunglasses, summer dresses, beautiful shoes, much too expensive. We had taken along bags full of nonsense: books that we didn't read and games that we didn't get to. We lay on the beach with the Italians and read to each other from *Privé*, *Story*, and *Weekend*. I tried to explain who TV personality Henny Huisman was. I even sang in the restaurant, accompanied by an old waiter playing an electric piano. I was able to sleep so well. No fear that the creep from the café would suddenly ring the doorbell. Just research on tanning agents and nail problems. If only I were still in Ancona. With Maria. On the beach in the evening. Next to each other, slightly sunburned and glowing. Looking at the sea.

She's been my best friend for more than ten years. Once we had a fight because I kissed a boy she liked. It was unbearable. I wanted to do anything to make up, that's how unhappy I was. A real girlfriend is a beacon, a house in the fog. That's what Maria is for me.

Looks into the garden, walks slowly through the room.

Yet everything will change. We grow. Unintentionally, insidiously. Maria will find a man, perhaps have children. Or I. Because we keep wanting things, something will always change. I hate it. I hate it.

One time, when we were still small, Pete and I sat in the backseat of the car, the red duck; Mom was driving, perhaps to the woods for mushrooms because it was autumn, the trees were brown. Mom asked us how we wanted it to be later, when we were grown-up. I felt Pete's solid, high-spirited body next to me; I saw Mom's long wavy hair hanging over the back of her seat, and I said: "Like now. It has to stay now forever." While I said it, I knew that it wasn't true because I wanted to have breasts and a dress with a floor-length full skirt, and I wanted to use mascara to make my eyelashes black—but it was also the truth. I wanted us to ride around forever in the warm car on the road to something we were looking forward to, and talk, tell stories, sing songs. Now forever.

Eat! Is there anything to eat?

Looks in the kitchen cupboards, opens the refrigerator.

Omelet? Toasted ham and cheese sandwich? Broiled open-faced sandwiches made Swedish style? What a blessing that those Spaniards finally cleared out, otherwise we would have had to cook an elaborate meal. Or go out for dinner without money. It's my fault. One of them thought he could get in bed with me last night. We had a great time dancing and partying in Paradiso, but I wanted to go to bed. I had to work today. I saw it coming; I went to sleep in Peter's room on the top floor with the door locked. They were staying downstairs on my floor, on camping mattresses. I heard them come home; for a moment I was afraid that the café monster had come in, but then I heard Spanish whispering on the stairs. And yes, there it was: "Sara, I come to you, we make love, yes?"

I couldn't bear to think about it! All of it was complicated enough. I acquired my foreign friends when we all studied in Stockholm for a year. It was party time every day and everyone was really nice and interesting. Of course we were drunk all the time. Our encounters when everyone was home again were often disappointing. Changes.

"No way, I am sleeping already," I shouted behind the barricaded door, "you go to sleep too! Sweet dreams!"

He slunk off, but his pride was so wounded that he packed his backpack the next morning. As did his comrade. Oh well. Too bad. Now I have an evening by myself.

Meanwhile she prepares something to eat and to drink, and sits down on the couch with it. Turns on the lamp, it is getting dark. Picks up the cell phone, holds it in her hands and reflects.

And now—Kevin. Call him or not? Did I do something wrong? I think so. He had bought tickets for the stadium, for Saturday. And it was Lea's birthday—I absolutely wanted to go there. I had to. A double commitment. Mom always says that many things resolve themselves. If you arrange something with Kevin, he usually calls right before to change plans. That leaves you standing in the kitchen in front of your Moroccan couscous, stamping your feet with rage.

That's not how it went Saturday. He was furious that I left at half-time, and I was angry that he didn't understand that I had to keep my promise to Lea. I ran to the subway station, which was completely deserted. I couldn't help crying with anger. He thinks that he has control over my schedule; I have to be ready when he is. I also cried because it's so difficult, because I make such a mess of things, because I'm unable to say coolly and clearly: "This evening I'm doing this and not that, with this person and not with that person." Well-organized. Be able to say no.

I've known him for ages, Kevin. From parties at school. Have even sung in his band. He's very funny. He always says something different from what you expect. He reads every word in magazines, just like me, and he also loves *Sesame Street* songs. I have always been attracted by the fact that he tries to do what he wants to. A good example. Now I see that a bit differently. I should never have fallen in love with him. Now I'll lose him doubly.

It went naturally; I wasn't aware of anything. We were simply good friends. Then his sister died. Suddenly. Of an illness that no one had noticed. Just like that, bam, dead. She was only twenty. I barely knew her. She and Kevin weren't as close to each other as Pete and I; there was probably too great a difference in age between them. I would go crazy if Pete died. Kevin didn't go crazy. Or he was already. He just continued working and didn't talk about anything. He was very cool. He made jokes as if nothing was the matter. Weird.

I went to the funeral with Maria and Lea and Heleen. Kim was there too. She has also known Kevin for a very long time. It seemed like a school reunion, all these people from our past strolling in front of the cemetery gate. There was a small jetty on the river side. Three musicians unpacked their instruments and started tuning. Violin, tuba, clarinet. The open cases lay at their feet.

It was sunny autumn weather, without wind. The reeds stood straight up along the river bank. People came and stood in a half circle around the landing, and the clarinet started to play a tune. The tuba supported it with arpeggios, and the violin's ethereal second part floated up. The song traveled over the very still water. We stood stock-still.

Then a black boat approached from a distance. The puffing of the motor blended with the music. At about sixty feet from the bank the captain turned off the motor. He was a young man with black curls, in black trousers and a black denim jacket. He walked forward over the gangway with a stick in his hand.

The musicians played a slow piece with gradually shifting chords. Everyone looked at the coffin which lay high on the boat, in the middle. Plain wood in the low sun. Flowers on top. Kevin's sister inside. Then the music stopped, the boat moored, and the pallbearers took a step forward. They lowered their heads to greet the coffin.

I had to cry so hard that it frightened me. It pushed up in my chest; I couldn't stop it. I walked to the gate and leaned against the wall. Distance. I saw the coffin lifted up and move slowly through the crowd. People drew back. Someone makes a last journey, goes across the earth before lying forever in the earth in her permanent place. And we know that. We greet her. Feel awe that someone dared to die. And fear. Fear.

The musicians played again and followed the coffin which moved, almost dancing, on the shoulders of the pallbearers. I joined the cortege.

Shivers, looks in the closet and pulls on a heavy colorful sweater. Sits down on the sofa, feet on the floor, looking straight ahead.

The confusion began in the weeks after the funeral. Time and again I had to think of that great wide sky above the still river, of the sound of our shuffling feet on the gravel, of the poignant ensemble of tuba and clarinet. And of the coffin which moved slowly, ever so slowly, to the grave.

I saw Kevin day and night. We watched rented videos and ate pizzas as if nothing had happened

If you can't talk, you have to listen to music. Music says something without words. A piece of music can express feelings that are too vague or too painful to capture in words. Or too awful.

I played music for him. Old soul numbers, Marvin Gaye, Otis Redding. The aria from the *Goldberg Variations*, Mozart's *Requiem*. He started to talk. To cry. He cracked. I was so directed toward him, to what he felt and said, that I didn't watch myself. I held him tightly when he shook with sobs. I kissed him. Kissed him again. Stroking suddenly became caressing. Before I knew it, sobbing had turned into giggling and we were making love. I did it, I was there, but what was I feeling, what did I think of it?

I wasn't thinking about that. "You're in love," said Maria. It wasn't true until then. Of course, I thought only of him. I practically didn't eat anymore. I floated. I didn't even care about that shitty office anymore.

We bicycled to the cemetery and wandered around among the gravestones. A stonecutter was on his knees, chiseling a tombstone. Faint tapping followed us. Next we lay down in the grass along the river. How can it be that you fall in love with someone whom you've known for years? I told Kim. She was shocked. She was worried about our group of friends. "If you break up you won't want to see him again, and what will become of us?"

I told Mom, who worried about me. "That boy is mourning. He doesn't really know what he is feeling. You are his life preserver. Watch out that you don't get swept along too much."

That was easy for her to say. I had no power over it. It made me angry that they all thought of themselves or how it was for me, and not of him, of his sorrow, of his loss.

Pulls her sweater more tightly around her, pulls up her legs, and wraps her arms around her knees.

My task was to think of his sorrow. He simply lived. He had to go to Antwerp for his work, and I imagined him sitting alone in a hotel room. "Follow him," said my kind office colleague. I had told him everything. Kevin had even come with me one time so that I could show him the horrors of office life in all its coarseness. I dropped everything and jumped onto the train. I called Mom from Antwerp. I was afraid that she'd start in with psychological talk, but she said: "Sweetheart, how wonderful for you, enjoy it."

Well, that isn't too helpful either. Did I want her to say: come home, I forbid this, break off with that boy? I'm twenty-seven. I should know what I'm doing.

The doubts started even then.

She shakes loose her long hair, gets up.

He was restless. Withdrawn. But it was also wonderful. Together. Undisturbed. Until his cell phone rang again, of course. Throw that thing away, I should have shouted. Actually, there were ups and downs. Harmony and exasperation. That continued once we were back. It became worse.

Straightens things up, walks around, looks into the garden, starts doing the dishes.

So many friends, and I have to see them all. Get-togethers. Traditions. Never refuse, because it is part of me, that web of friendship is my nature. "One note on the piano is nothing," Mom said one time, "that's simply a question of weight on a key; it makes no difference whether it's a lead marble or the finger of Richter. But two notes or more! It isn't until a connection develops with other notes that that one note attains its character."

Kevin and I created an awfully strange harmony. The kind of

chord that can wobble to any side; it doesn't resolve in the end and goes nowhere.

I'm going to do my nails.

Looks in her backpack for her nail polish, starts painting her toenails intently.

Every time when I thought: now we're through it, now things will calm down and be normal, something would happen—a forgotten date, a refused night, a bluntness that shocked me. But every time there was also the reconciliation, the song that we'd start singing at the same time, the shared longing for the river.

My nails give me away. They indicate my state of mind. I work hard on them. No biting. Filing. Nourishing lotion. Massaging them. Pushing back the cuticles, with the cuticle tool. Despite the crisis, they've been looking good lately. Well-groomed. Adult!

Then he wanted out. "OK," I said, "there's such confusion, we'll simply not see each other for half a year. After that we'll decide." Thought it was pretty mature of myself. Except that it didn't work at all because we did see each other of course, and he missed me and wanted me to go with him to the cemetery, and I longed for him, and we went back and forth under those dappled sycamores, among the sagging graves with old cries of distress on them, to his sister's fresh grave—I really felt for him; I was willing to give up everything to make his sorrow bearable.

He left me in the lurch at a party. I'd waited for him for hours, and when he got there nothing was right; he wanted no contact and pushed me away when I put my arm around his neck. I went home with Maria. We dragged her mattress in front of the television; I lay there crying and fell asleep.

At that point something changed. I no longer counted on him. I was still there when he was sad; I went with him to the movies when he asked, but I remained at a distance. It wasn't as controlled as it seems, otherwise I wouldn't have started carrying on with that crazy guy from the café. But I didn't touch my nails. They grew. I forced myself to go to work, no matter how awful that was. I was little Miss Sunshine there. "It's so boring here; please, Sara, sing a song for us," said the senior manager. Then I'd jump on a desk and sing. A stern woman from personnel said that things had become more enjoyable since I worked there. They were happy with me. That was good for me.

I am. I exist. I'm still tanned from Italy.

Just now, on the way home, I bicycled past Kim's. She came out of her house, and we stopped to talk on the street for a moment. "I won't do it any longer," I said, "I'm now going to live myself." She nodded.

The cell phone rings. She looks for it, finds it, puts it to her ear, listens.

—Oh. Yes! That's great!
—Yes, I'll do that. Will I receive it by mail?
—Thank you very much. Yes, till next week.

Jumps up, throws the cell phone on the couch, dances.

Yes! Yes! Yes! Super-Sara, the terror of the freshman class! I did it! "You're at the top of our list," he said—the director or the principal, or whatever that character is called. Now I'm a teacher. And no one knows it yet. Never again to the office. A farewell in the cafeteria with presents and messy pastries and speeches. Tomorrow I'll dress fabulously. A dress.

Looks through the clothes closet and pulls out a beautiful summer dress.

Yes, this is the one. Mom isn't here anyway. I'll take this one with me.

She holds the dress in front of her body, swaying her hips. Lays it ready on the couch.

I had applied secretly. As if I were ashamed. Not a singing career. Not a dazzling TV anchor. Not a witty journalist. A teacher.

It isn't at all what I want, and yet I'm happy. When I was little I wanted to become a teacher. I placed Peter with his fat behind in a small chair and read to him: "*The Bremen Town Musicians*." Very slowly. I had just learned to read. He had to write letters and learn songs. He did all of it.

Now I've managed to do something all by myself. Perhaps it isn't much, but it's mine. I should really start phoning people right away: Peter, Maria, Kim, Kevin, Dad, and Mom. Found my life's fulfillment. The search is over.

Next week fly to Mom and Dad. Prepare my lessons at a lake in Sweden.

No. I won't call. Not tonight. I can be content by myself. It isn't necessary to have everyone shouting, "Well done." No.

I have a life. A note that is mine. I don't have to rush-rush to join in the chords of others, to watch out that I don't disrupt their harmony, to clear out in time to leave the melody to another. I can establish my own tempo, sing a constant part that the others can join or not. Calm. Not be frightened of a dissonance here or there. I determine it myself. It doesn't always have to be a brilliant solo voice. You can hear it anyway because it is *my* voice. It's mine. And I am Sara.

Put away the mess.
Put back the sweater.
Close the garden doors.
Turn off the light. Sleep. Sleep.

The lights go out. After some time: lights as in the beginning.

I went upstairs and fell into a deep, peaceful sleep in my old room. Behind the open window, the apple trees stood motionless in the night. The headlights of a car late at night shone through a chink in the curtains and formed a slowly moving train of light against the ceiling. Were turned off. The motor stopped. A car door slammed closed. Footsteps. Silence. Downstairs I knew where to find the photo albums with our whole life inside them. Mom had managed to paste in the graduation party before she went on vacation. Everything, everything caught in photos. Birthdays, of course, always with the same cakes, Saint Nicholas celebrations around the laundry basket filled with presents, Lucia celebrations, vacations. Our playroom. The bunk beds. Dad carrying me on his shoulders. Pete and me as piano soloists on two baby grands. Album after album I materialize. Dad and Mom become increasingly tired and gray, one heavier and the other thinner. I appear in these photos until I am present-day Sara. And everything in between is there. They stand in the closet.

The alarm stood glowing on the desk. It would go off a little before seven. I'd have to get out of bed to turn it off. I turned over and slept.

I appeared more brave and more independent than I was. I had not only gone to my parents' home to rest. I had not only canceled my dinner date with Heleen and Maria to pull myself together. I was exhausted, certainly. My body was spent and needed rest. Nourishment.

I had also gone to the home of my youth because I was afraid in my own house. I wanted to be among the familiar furniture to be reassured. I needed to smell the garden, to borrow one of Mom's dresses, to eat from my childhood plate.

That was not brave. But I did it. For whatever reason. I was alone one evening and one night and I was satisfied with what there was. How it was. No panic, no rebelliousness, no euphoria. Peace and quiet.

When I woke up the sky was still pale, but when I stepped out of the shower the sky was sheer blue above the houses. No clouds, no wind. My toenails were magnificently polished. It was almost pitiful to stick them in the gray sneakers. I put on my bicycling clothes and put the beautiful dress and the party shoes in the backpack. I was going to outdo myself for the last time. They were really going to miss me there in September!

I made coffee; I ate a rusk; I took time for everything. When I was finished, I surveyed the room. Plates and cups were drying on the kitchen counter. The table was wiped clean.

From the stack of mail I fished the postcard that I had sent to my parents from Italy. I placed it in the middle of the table. Nonsense, for I would go to see them next week and the three of us would come home together. I wanted to put my stamp on the room. I had been here, in this house, where I knew every wall and every baseboard, and I had made a decision. Alone. By myself.

I pushed my bicycle outside and double-locked the door.

Bicycling went almost automatically. Especially now that I could be found in the gym almost daily. My legs, sturdy muscle pillars, pedaled me almost effortlessly onto the dike. From our house you can ride to the city along the water. They say that you have to walk in order to really see and experience everything around you. When you walk you have the right pace. Everything that your senses soak up can go straight into your brain. They can reveal so much. I wanted speed. I wanted to whoosh past the world; I wanted houses, bushes, and parks to light up in the corners of my eyes and then be left behind while I zoomed by. I made good speed on the straight piece of road next to the canal.

In the shadow of the willows, drops of dew still lay on the grass. I breathed in the fresh chill air, but already felt the sun on my back and my shoulders. A fisherman was sitting on the bank. When I had passed him I started singing.

Blue, gray, green. Sky, paving stones, grass. At the start of spring, all greens are different: pale, yellowy, silvery, mossy. In the middle of the summer, those distinctions are gone, and trees, bushes, and plants are an even, saturated green. On the banks stood the enormous leaves of wild rhubarb between fans of cow parsley. Yellow flowers, white flowers, blue flowers. Between the stones of the bike path grew that plant that you can use to cure mosquito bites. The leaves with their elongated veins lay spread out flat on the pavement. I could no longer remember its name. You have to crush the leaf and rub the sap over the lump. Away with the itch. Ribworth Plantain. That was it.

Would I be satisfied as a teacher? Did I have to be? Of course not. I would go and do it the way I was. Then it wouldn't be bad if I didn't know something. Next week I would go and pick up the books and then carefully prepare the lessons for the first period. Request class lists, with comments from the previous teacher. I wanted to know my students before they saw me. Hand in cell phones before the class. No chewing gum. No coats. It was a part-time job; I had enough time to start something else in addition. Good, very good.

In the middle of the canal sailed a boat. A small boy was playing in a playpen on the deck. The light was so bright that I could see his fire truck with its silver ladder. His mother was cleaning the wooden deck with a mop that she dipped into the water from time to time. She waved its dripping tip back and forth above the child's head; he reached for the drops with both hands. I heard him shriek with laughter.

Tall façades. Houseboats. A first terrace—still empty.

I could go and work as a volunteer for immigrants' television or with the children's broadcasting in the hospital. If that went well and I had learned something, then I could go and apply for a job with real television. Not with giant leaps but step by step, just as I was now bicycling into the city. Calm and purposeful.

The streets started getting crowded. Everyone was bicycling because the weather was so beautiful. I turned away from the water and into the narrow street toward the city center. My watch was in the outside pocket of my backpack; I wanted to have solidly tanned arms. I also didn't care what time it was. I took my time. So what if I arrived fifteen minutes later at that office.

Pay attention. Cars. They're in a hurry. Mom always said that you have to make eye-contact with the driver—that way you know that he's seen you too. When Peter returns from his vacation, I'll have a real job, I thought. Then he'll be proud of me, just as I am of him. After work we'll sit and smoke on our balcony and talk about our day. Watch how the evening falls in the backyards. Drink a beer.

Almost eight-thirty on the clock of the palace. I would never manage to get there on time, according to the clock. Carefully I moved alongside an enormous white truck that was waiting at the stoplight. I wanted to get past it. Stopped with one foot on the curb. In front of me the palace was glittering in the sun. Pigeons. One of these dumb living statues that frightens children when it moves suddenly. Tourists already waiting in line in front of the museum entrance. I waited as well, calm and composed, until the light turned green.

Then I pushed off quickly to shoot past the palace like a spear. Something touched my rear wheel; I lost my balance; I fell. Sharp, small stones. A crashing, swelling roar. A strange weight came over me; I heard fiercely rustling woods, or was it water, a giant foaming waterfall that rang in my ears; I looked at the water mass with Mom, Dad, and Peter; we were drenched; it seemed as if we were standing in a fountain, and the water pelted and beat and battered and buried us—we shouted with excitement and held one another's hands between the water curtains with rainbows inside them and the sun; the sun burned through the water and it became whiter and whiter until the light exploded in my head and a shining wall was going to crush me, and I squeezed Peter's hand, and we laughed, we roared with laughter.

In the middle of the square. And I am Sara.

Lights are suddenly turned off, for at least twenty seconds. Then house lights.

Acknowledgments

Alma" was commissioned by the Rotterdam Philharmonic Gergiev Festival. The monologue was performed on September 19, 2002, by Fania Sorel, and preceded a performance of Gustav Mahler's Sixth Symphony in the Doelen concert hall in Rotterdam.

The monologue is based to a large extent on historical facts as described in letters and diaries. I have used the following literature:

Giroud, Françoise: *Alma Mahler ou l'art d'être aimée*; Editions Robert Laffont, Paris 1988.

Lalande, Françoise: *Alma Mahler*; Actes Sud—Papiers, Paris 1989.

Mahler, Alma: *Het is een vloek een meisje te zijn* [It is a curse to be a girl]; De Arbeiderspers, Amsterdam 2000.

Mahler, Alma: *Mijn Leven* [My life]; De Arbeiderspers, Amsterdam 1989.

Mahler, Gustav: *Symphony No. 6* [score]; Eulenburg, Mainz 1968.

Nebehay, Christian: *Wien Speziell*, Musik um 1900 [Vienna 1900]; Brandstätter, Vienna 1984.

Schorske, Carl: *Wenen in het Fin-de-Siècle* [Fin-de-Siècle Vienna]; Agon, Amsterdam 1989.

"Cato and Leendert" and "Mendel Bronstein" were written for the production *Lazarus* as part of Rotterdam Cultural Capital of Europe in 2001. The project was conceived and produced by Peter Sonneveld. The monologues were performed by Aafke Buringh, Ruurt De Maesschalck, and Paul Röttger in the summer of 2001. These monologues were also based on historical sources:

Laar, Paul van de: *Stad van formaat. Geschiedenis van Rotterdam in de 19e and 20e eeuw* [A great city: the history of Rotterdam in the 19th and 20th century], vol. 2; Waanders Uitgevers, Zwolle 2000.

"The Doctor" was commissioned by the Bonheur theater company. It was produced in the spring of 2005 for the commemoration of the bombing of Rotterdam in 1940. The monologue was performed by Ruurt De Maesschalck.

Baarda, Frits: *Uit het Hart, Rotterdammers over het bombardement* [From the Heart: Citizens of Rotterdam about the Bombing]: Focus/SDU Uitgeverij, Amsterdam/Den Haag 1990.

About the Author

Anna Enquist

Anna Enquist is a musician, a psychoanalyst, a poet and a novelist. One of the best-loved writers of her native Holland, she is also a best-selling author in Germany, Switzerland, France, Sweden and Austria. Her first collection of poetry won the award for new Dutch poetry—the prestigious C. Buddingh' prize—and has been followed by four more collections of poetry, all of which have gone back to press frequently. Her novels have achieved similar acclaim; *The Masterpiece*, *The Secret* and *The Ice Carriers* all proved to be runaway bestsellers, each with over 250,000 copies sold. *The Secret* won the 1997 Dutch Readers' Prize. All are available from *The* Toby Press.

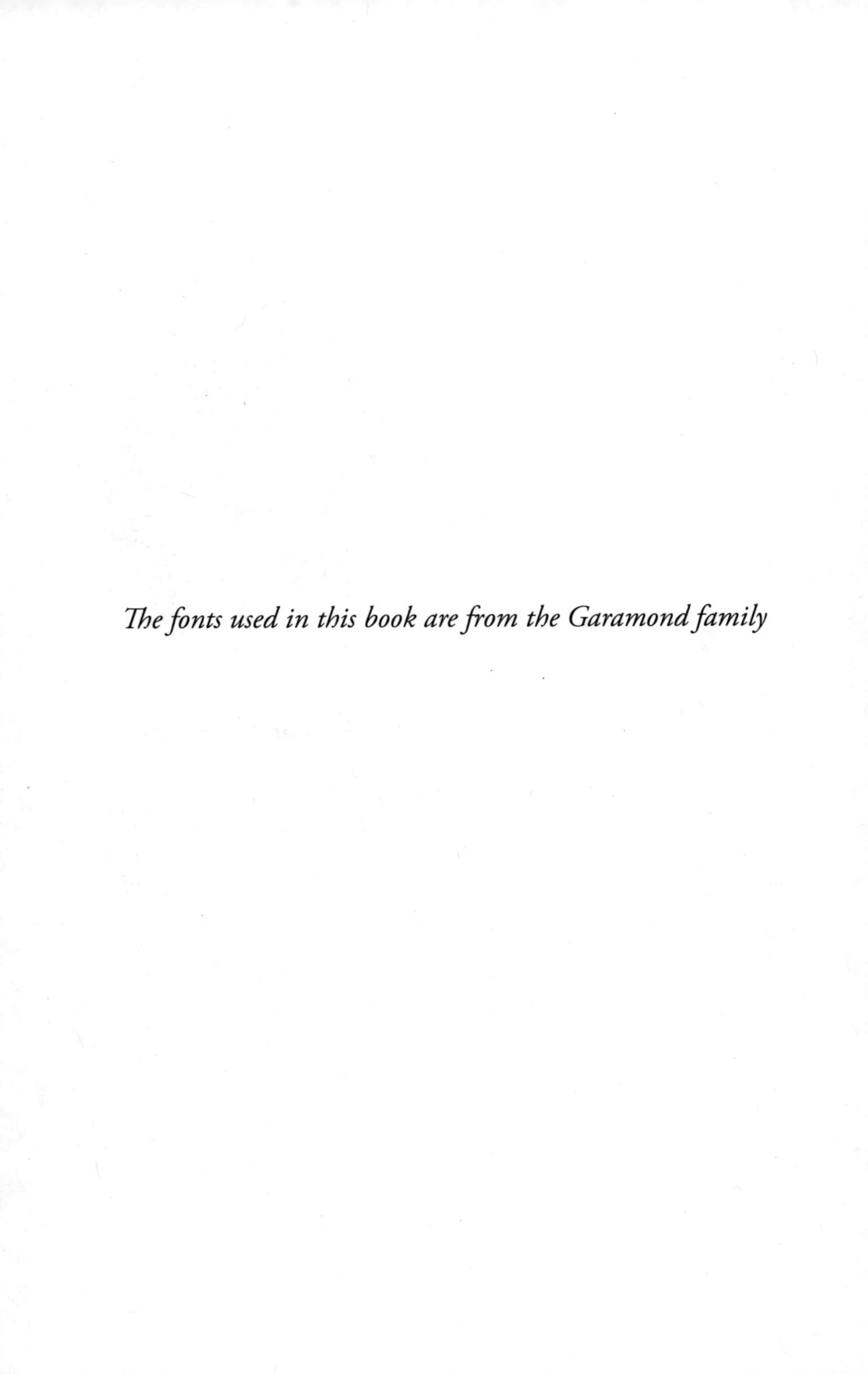

The fonts used in this book are from the Garamond family

Other works by Anna Enquist
available from *The* Toby Press

The Fire was Here

The Ice Carriers

The Injury

The Masterpiece

The Secret

The Toby Press publishes fine writing,
available at leading bookstores everywhere. For more
information, please visit www.tobypress.com